They could make beautiful music together…

Hoping to dodge a scandal that could destroy her personal life and her career, Alex fled grad school for a summer job in tiny Potterville, West Virginia. She didn't expect the town cupids to orchestrate a "chance" meeting with Marc—a sexy, brooding rock star who appreciates her love of poetry. But Alex doubts he'll want anything more if he discovers the indiscretion she can't forgive herself for…

Marc came to Potterville to get some space from his band and clear his head. But before he knows it, he's intrigued with the waitress at the local diner. Alex is not only smart and beautiful, she's inspiring his songwriting and taking it to the next level. Soon he's falling for her—and then she runs away. For the first time, Marc is chasing after a woman—and giving both himself and Alex a chance to heal past hurts and take a chance on the future…

Visit us at www.kensingtonbooks.com

Books by Christa Maurice

Drawn to the Rhythm Series
Satellite of Love
Heaven Beside You
Waiting For A Girl Like You

Arden FD Series
Three Alarm Tenant
Struck By Lightning
Spark of Desire

Weaver's Circle Series
Secrets Everybody Knows
Long Memory

One Ring to Rule
Melody Unchained

Published by Kensington Publishing Corporation

Waiting For A Girl Like You

Drawn to the Rhythm Series

Christa Maurice

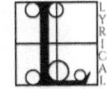

LYRICAL PRESS
Kensington Publishing Corp.
www.kensingtonbooks.com

To all the university employees who were willing to indulge in "what if" conversations.

Chapter 1

"Alex, I'm switching you and Tina." Ida touched her shellacked hair.

"Okay, tomorrow I'll start outside." Alex headed away from the register. Half an hour and she was off for the day. About damn time. The gravy that the adorable, little darling dumped on her apron at the beginning of lunch was starting to crack as it dried, and the weight of today's tips would have her walking with a tilt.

"No, I mean now."

Big-haired, thick-waisted, hometown charm Ida was not kidding. Alex turned back. "Excuse me?"

"I need you to cover outside now."

Alex pursed her lips before she refused. Saying no last time had worked out so well that she might need to delete it from her vocabulary. "Why?"

"Because I want you to wait on Marc." Ida tapped one of her neon pink nails on the window. Alex could only assume she was pointing at the Marc under discussion, but didn't care enough to look. She should never have said the day could only get better. Tempting fate, it was. Instead, she scanned her tables—her former tables. Three of them were about to get up, and Tina would decide they had to split all the tips, meaning Tina was going to clean up while Alex got the short end of the stick.

And none of this was worth arguing about.

"Fine. Did you tell Tina?"

"I will after I pick up them tables getting ready to go." Proving Ida wasn't a complete ogre. She'd make sure Alex got her tips, at least. That still didn't answer what Alex had done wrong to be sentenced to work on the patio.

Alex went outside. Tina was nowhere to be seen, which was why her tips sucked. Alex cruised the tables. Of the ten tables that composed Tina's section, eight needed something. Table nine was happy, but running low on drinks and roughly ten minutes from finishing. At table ten, the guy was on the phone.

"Well, Dez, I guess you should have hooked up with a lawyer instead of a personal trainer." He scowled, looking dark and dangerous. Thin, long legs, and shaggy dark hair. The kind of guy who would have made her heart go pitter-pat when she was sweet little sixteen, but she wasn't a sweet little anything anymore. Roger took care of the last of that. The bastard.

"No. Not another dime." The man at the table said into the phone. "The sucker bank is closed."

Sucker bank. Good one. Alex gestured at the bare table, nothing but the daisy in the little vase in the center and a half empty sugar caddy.

The guy shook his head. "How many times do I have to say no before you believe me?"

Alex mouthed that she'd be back. He at least needed a place setting and water.

Drew met up with her at the drink station. "Sorry, I've been trying to keep up, but I can't do two sections, and Tina is on another break." The alfresco seating at Ida's Diner used to be a mechanic's garage so the seating was in the bays and on the cement apron out front and the drink station was in the former office. Very kitschy and cute like the rest of the town. Drew had the nine tables in the old service bay. "What did you do to get exiled out here?"

"No idea. Ida just told me I had to switch. I'm off in a half hour, anyway. Can you prep me five glasses of water?"

"Sure thing."

Alex made a round with utensils, napkins, and straws. Table Ten was still on the phone, but not smoking, just playing with the cigarette. He didn't look like he was about to commit a felony anymore either, just a misdemeanor.

"What I'm asking you is how she got this number." He twiddled the cigarette between his fingers like a tiny baton. "That's not an answer."

Alex arranged utensils on the placemat. A new conversation.

"Jody, listen to me very carefully. Client information is privileged. You don't give it out to anybody. If they don't have it already, they don't need it. I am the client. We don't want to have to let you go, but this is a serious infraction." He mashed the cigarette on the table.

Alex shuddered. Table Ten was going to fire this Jody person over the phone. What an asshole.

"No, Candy will not be able to save your ass this time. Candy understands how important it is for the public to not have my private number even when that particular member of the public used to be married to me. Plus, Candy is in China picking out a child."

Drew probably had that water ready. She needed to get it delivered. How bad an infraction was it to give out a phone number to somebody he already knew? Maybe it was worse when you had friends who went to China to pick out children.

"Jody, she's my ex-wife for a reason, and she already soaked me for six million dollars."

Six million dollars? Alex reappraised Table Ten. Jeans, but good jeans. T-shirt featuring a guitar and a snake—must be a concert shirt. Wristwatch. Wait. Tag Hauer wristwatch.

"Jody, Jody, please stop crying." Table Ten caught Alex's eye and frowned.

Shit. Busted. Alex opened her hands in a menu gesture to cover for why she was hanging around the table. This was a restaurant and he didn't have a menu in his hands. Two and two made a perfect excuse.

Table Ten shook his head and mouthed, "Paul."

Ida had shifted her out here to wait on this guy, the cook knew his standing order, he had an ex-wife who had "soaked" him for six million dollars, a Tag Hauer watch, and some sort of administrative assistant. The hair was too long for the average businessman, and the jeans were too trendy and expensive for a politico or a tourist. Therefore, Marc at table ten was somebody very exclusive sitting at a diner in Potterville, West Virginia.

Nothing in this town fit. When her cousin Angela said she could make a mint in tips waiting tables over the summer in this little tourist town that didn't seem to have any special draw outside of the landscape, Alex hadn't believed her, yet a mint she was making.

The waters Drew prepped for her had been sitting long enough to sweat. She dropped them off, careful not to linger at table ten. She was there long enough to pick up that he was now talking to Tessa about Jody giving his number to Dez, the ex-wife, who soaked him for the six million dollars. Not that money was the main goal of her life, but one had to pause when numbers like that started flying around.

"Hey, Paul." She pushed through the kitchen door. "There's a guy at—"

"I know. Marc." Paul gave a little shiver of excitement as he pushed a plate across the service table. "Take him this plate."

Alex pointed at it. "This plate."

"Yes, this plate."

"This very plate."

Paul shook his finger at her. "Don't get sassy with me."

Alex grinned. Paul was yet another thing that didn't fit. A world-class chef cooking at a diner in the West Virginian mountains. Maybe Marc with the Tag Hauer came for Paul. In a past life, Paul had been a chef in New York and had followed Cassandra Geoffrey here when she moved back after her divorce, but Cassie was now remarried and living in California either all the time or most of the time. Angela hadn't been too clear.

The plate looked like five-star quality. Mushroom sauce trailed artfully over a thick, juicy steak. The baked potato should have been on the cover of a magazine. The crisp, golden skin split to allow a perfect square of rich yellow butter to melt into the fluffy mash with a sprinkling of fresh chives over top. The herbs had been clipped just this morning from the garden Paul maintained in his backyard. The salad balanced in such a perfect tower that Alex wasn't sure she'd get it to the table without having it topple over. A crystal wine glass filled with jewel-toned red wine completed the meal. More incongruities. Ida's didn't serve wine, and they didn't serve anything in crystal. Everybody else in the place was drinking out of old Mason jars.

Maybe Paul would cook up this meal for her one day if she asked nice.

At table ten, the cigarette was gone and Marc was on yet a different phone conversation. At least she assumed it was a different conversation since he referred to the person on the other end as man three times while Alex set out his meal. He was smiling now and beamed at her when she finished. A standard thank-you beam of someone too busy to speak to the help, but something about it shot down her spine with electric heat and triggered an insipid smile in return.

Oh, God.

All her tables were good for the moment, so Alex ducked into the ladies room in the garage. Ten minutes left before she could hang up her gravy-stained, crackling apron for the day. She washed her hands and her face before stopping to examine herself. Dilated eyes, flushed cheeks— maybe she was coming down with something. After work she could head back to Angela and Finn's and let her cousin fuss over her.

She rounded the tables again, but dinner was ending, so more people were heading out than seating, which lightened the workload. Through the restaurant window, she could see Ida pouring on the local flavor at the register and Paul circulating tables, receiving his laurels. Marc at table ten was either still or again on the phone with his meal untouched.

"I just wanted you to know what happened, Sandy."

Dez, Jody, Tessa, Sandy—the man was awash in women.

"I have to go. If I don't have this steak at least half eaten before Paul gets here, he'll cry or something." Marc picked up his knife. "Yeah. Yeah. Bye, Sandy." He tapped the disconnect button on his Bluetooth. "Don't ever get married."

"What?" Alex stopped in the act of taking his empty water glass.

"Never mind. How are you?"

"Me?"

"Yes, you." He cut into the steak. "Paul is an artist."

"He is. Enjoy your dinner." Alex turned away from the table, intent on turning over the remainder of her tables to Drew and getting out of here.

"Aren't you going to answer the question?" Marc asked.

Alex turned back. Potterville should change its name to Incongruity, West Virginia. "I thought it was rhetorical."

"No. How are you? Enjoying working here for the summer? You are just here for the summer, aren't you? I don't remember seeing you before."

"Yes, I… My cousin lives in town, and she told me I could earn a lot of money waiting tables here. The tips are really good." Alex clutched her hands together, hoping it would anchor her to reality. So far, no good.

"Who's your cousin?" He forked a bite of steak into his mouth.

"Angela Runningwater."

"Mm." He nodded like that fit something together for him. Heaven only knew what, but since this was Incongruity, West Virginia, it could be anything. Or nothing.

She tried to pull off a professional smile, but it felt broken. "Enjoy your dinner."

Drew was at the drink station when she got there. "Almost time."

Alex checked her watch, a cheap little number she'd fished out of a bargain bin at a Big Lots. It kept time. That's all she needed it for. "Past time, sucker. They're all yours. This is table ten." She shoved the glass at him.

"The *special* table."

"Exactly." She emptied her tips into her purse and tossed the dirty apron into the hamper. "See you tomorrow."

"Bye."

Instead of going past the front of the restaurant, Alex ducked behind and walked down the street toward Angela and Finn's house. Tourists stuck to the main drag. The restaurant, the churches, the library, the elementary school, the square. All the stuck-in-time, Americana Main Street they came to indulge in. They didn't tend to wander into the neighborhoods behind so much. It would be too much like going backstage at Disneyland.

The night was turning out nice. Clear and breezy. All week it had been sweltering hot, which was why she preferred to work inside the air-conditioned restaurant, and why Tina had been stuck with the concrete patio. Do good work, get rewarded. That was the theory. Alex licked her lips. Marc at table ten would make for a great reward. *No, no, don't go there.* Some things are better off as a mystery. She wanted to crawl in bed with Percy Bysshe Shelley. She'd been trying to finish that biography for a week now.

* * * *

"Well, what do you think?" Paul asked.

"Spectacular as always, Paul."

"She is lovely, isn't she?"

Marc glanced at his half-eaten steak. Was Paul getting chummy with the food now? Ida would blow a gasket if he wanted to change the restaurant to vegetarian. "She?"

"Alex. Your waitress. I told Ida she had to send Alex out to wait your table."

The matchmakers were at it. Marc drew a deep breath while the information settled around his shoulders. Better than Paul going vegetarian at least. "Is that so? I'm pretty sure I can find women on my own."

"I'm sure you can. You could walk into the middle of the street and throw a rock and come up with a dozen, but nobody wants to see you make another mistake like Desiree."

"I was divorced from her long before I met you."

"And you've been through half a dozen since who were just not suitable." Paul put his hands on his hips. "You need to get laid by someone who isn't looking at your bank balance, and if there's anyone, it's Alex. She isn't what you'd call a material girl."

Right. She'd made the comment about coming here to make money. Of course, she was talking about tips, not fishing for diamonds and Bentleys. "Paul, I came to town to relax."

"If you wanted to relax, you wouldn't be in the one town on the planet where you were most likely to be recognized."

"I could be recognized anywhere."

Paul poked the table with one straightened finger. "People come to Potterville hoping to see a member of Touchstone. We can read you, boy-o. You want companionship." Paul slid into the chair across the table. "Keep eating while I lecture you."

"Okay." Marc cut into his steak. "You've been spending too much time with Ida."

"Now, I know Alex isn't your normal type," Paul began, ignoring Marc's comment. "She's a bit on the slender side, but she's very bright, and she deserves a break. She's working on a master's degree and pinching every penny along the way. Angela says she had a boyfriend, but there was something scandalous about it, and she broke up with him. Right now, she's in the perfect place for a nice summer fling. And for that job, you, my dear, are an ideal candidate."

"Got this all planned out, do you?" A summer fling wouldn't be a hardship, and this Alex girl wasn't hard on the eyes, either. If he did it right, they could part as friends at the end. Unlike Jason who tried to have a fling and ended up married to the girl. Not that Cassie was a disaster. Cassie was probably the luckiest thing that had happened to the band since Candy made friends with Ronnie Bauer's son, but Marc didn't plan to get married again anytime soon. Not until he got this Desiree thing taken care of, and that might require a hit man.

"Yes, we do. Right now, she's staying with Angela and Finn in that thimble Finn calls a house. We think you should invite her to stay in the guest cottage on the mountain."

"Why didn't you tell Cassie to do that?"

Paul flushed and turned away.

That was telling. Cassie had promised the house to Marc for the summer so he could play recluse if he wanted and still have adulation in easy reach. She wouldn't want to inflict some woman on him without permission. Paul and Ida wouldn't think twice, and they wouldn't stop until they succeeded. They played a long game.

"Just give her a try." Paul stood up. "Don't tell her it was a set up. She's even more prickly than you are."

"And if she's not interested?"

"Then I guess *you* are not all you're cracked up to be, sugar." Paul patted his cheek and walked away.

Paul was spending way too much time with Ida.

* * * *

"How was it tonight?" Angela asked before Alex crossed the threshold. She and Finn were sitting on the couch watching television like good, normal people. Since it was after nine, John-John must have been in bed.

Alex had not paused in her route across the living room toward the hall. Finn's weird OCD routines freaked her out, and she really needed to spend some quality time on her own mental health before she could deal with someone else's. Besides, she had to be invading their space. They were being very generous letting her stay, and she didn't want to be any more of a burden than necessary. "Pretty good. My purse weighs a ton so I'm going to be up late rolling coins."

"No! Marc! Did you meet Marc?" Angela leaped off the couch and bounded across the room like a soap bubble caught in a draft. "Ida said he was coming to town today and he eats at the diner every night when he's here."

Alex hurried down the hall like demons were pursuing her instead of her cousin. Everybody in town must be hung up on this guy. Cute. Okay, smoldering, but those were everywhere. "I guess so. Ida put me outside at the end of my shift, and I'm pretty sure it was just so I could wait on this Marc guy at table ten." She dropped her purse on the dresser in the guest room. It clinked and jingled as the coins inside rearranged themselves.

"Skinny? Dark hair? He's so cute, isn't he? And so nice. I never thought famous people would be so nice, but everybody in Jason's band are so nice." Angela flushed.

Alex wasn't sure if the flush was caused by her excitement or her grammatical error. No, it had to be the excitement. Which begged the question, why was she so excited about table ten? "What band?"

"Touchstone."

"Touchstone? Did they do that song 'Lucky Charmer'?"

"Yes." Angela nodded so fast that Alex expected her fillings to jingle as much as the coins in Alex's purse. "We told Cassie about you, and she agreed he would like you, and since you were going to be here waiting tables, and he was going to be here vacationing, it was perfect."

What was perfect?

"Cassie is always right about these things. She was right about me and Finn."

That was what was perfect. The entire town was conspiring to push her into the arms of this rock star. Alex drew a deep breath. If the entire town thought she should make a play for this not-so-bad-boy, she couldn't disappoint them. He was mighty nice to look at and, no doubt, better to touch. Plus, he had an added acceptability factor. Angela wouldn't be pushing her toward a married man. After being evasive about whom she was dating for the past three years, Alex needed a boyfriend her parents could meet. The fact that Marc was good looking and successful was a bonus. It wasn't all *Dirty Dancing* and "nobody puts Baby in the corner." And what was the worst that could happen? He wouldn't like her? Not everybody was going to like her according to the self-help books she'd been reading. All part of the journey.

She wouldn't mind if he liked her. That crack about the sucker bank and that he really wanted to know how she was upped his attractiveness by a factor of ten.

"I'll talk to him and see what happens."

"Yay!" Angela grabbed her in a typically overenthusiastic hug. "I have big news, too."

Alex shifted, testing her ribs as Angela released her. She hoped to get through the summer without broken bones, but she wouldn't bet on it. "Oh?"

"Finn says it's time for us to try for a little baby brother or sister for John-John." Angela blushed.

Once upon a time Alex had been that naive. Blushing at the thought of sex. Smiling when talking about her beloved. Believing that the one she loved wanted the best for her. Not that Finn didn't want the best for Angela. At least the best that was in his comfort zone to give. From the outside, their marriage looked a little automated and dull. Because she was the best judge of a solid relationship, after all.

"That's great. I'm happy for you."

"He doesn't like to—you know—do it when you're in the house, though." Angela blushed a deeper shade of crimson.

So far as Alex had been able to determine, Finn didn't like to do anything when she was in the house except sit on the couch and watch TV. Sometimes he would eat, but only at the prescribed meal times. She couldn't even recall him going to the bathroom when she was in the house. The poor man was going to end up with the world's worst case of constipation by the end of the summer. "No problem. I close a couple days a week, anyway. I'll just stay out extra late."

Angela sighed so heavily that Alex thought she might run out of oxygen and faint. "I knew you would understand. He makes me so happy. I hope you're as happy with Marc as I am with Finn."

Yes, because Marc was going to fall in love with her and sweep her away from all this. The Rock Star and the Waitress. It was like the plot of a penny dreadful, emphasis on dreadful. It couldn't hurt to try. Alex smiled. "Maybe."

Angela hugged her again, this time without causing Alex's ribs to creak, then hurried out to rejoin Old Reliable watching the never-ending parade of sitcoms and police procedural dramas.

Alex leaned back against the headboard for the best view of the door and the sliver of hall beyond. Maybe that was real love. The stable, permanent kind. All her life she'd been pursuing the sparks-flying, big band passion. What if it was just meatloaf on Monday and *CSI* on Tuesday with tongue *A* inserted into slot *B* every Saturday night? Or was *CSI* on Wednesdays? And if they were trying for another child, tongue *A* would be in slot *B* more frequently. Marc didn't inspire grand passion, but he was nice enough, funny, and good-looking. He was already more than she had the right to ask for. A better investment of her time might be figuring out what kind of woman she needed to be for him. He wasn't going to be attracted to an egghead lit major. If half the town wanted it, she should try her best. She'd done such a dandy job of choosing her own romantic partners; she should start outsourcing that task. Anybody could do a better job than she had.

* * * *

The next night, Alex sent the last customers off with a friendly good night. The air was hot and sticky, and she was looking forward to getting back to Angela's house, getting out of her horrible heels, and going to bed. She had spent the entire evening proving the adage about never wearing new shoes without breaking them in first. Although, they had earned their price tag in increased tips. Too bad Marc hadn't shown up to appreciate the effort. He was the whole reason for wearing them.

Two hours research last night, and another hour this morning, had yielded very little in results as to what he liked. Twenty years of photos of him with thin women in short skirts and high heels didn't reveal a lot. She had learned his favorite color was green, but she didn't own anything green, so that was a wash. And he liked sports, especially the big three: football, basketball, and baseball. Unfortunately, she knew nothing about sports of any kind so that wasn't an opening. The only useful piece of information she'd gleaned was that he appreciated his privacy, which she had learned last night, listening to him ream out that woman over the phone for giving out his number. Lacking anything that would give her a conversation opener, Alex had resorted to a pair of new heels and the shortest skirt she owned and decided to play dumb on who he was and a little hard to get. A man like that had to get tired of women throwing themselves at him. Not that she could blame them. Smart, funny, hot. Any woman on his arm would feel like she'd won the relationship lottery. Damn it, now she did want him to like her. Ida and Paul had both commented that she looked pretty tonight, and then fretted about the fact that Marc hadn't shown.

It gave her an excellent excuse to chicken out.

In the middle of clearing the table, she paused. Crap. She couldn't go back to Angela's straight away tonight. Not now that Finn had decided the time was right to have a second child and the necessary deed could not be executed with her in the other bedroom. He wouldn't consider a little afternoon delight, either.

Potterville didn't lack for options on Saturday night. The church was having a dance like always. Not with these feet. Robot wars were going on at the high school. Maybe. There was a play at the middle school. On the upside, it was *Midsummer Night's Dream*. On the downside, it was performed by middle schoolers. The bus had already left for stargazing at Dolly Sods Wilderness Area, so that was out. The surprisingly good high school band and glee club were performing in the town square, but they would be hitting the finale about now. The movie showing at the elementary school would be half over by the time she left, leaving that out, too. The ice cream stand would be hopping until midnight, which would provide a wonderful opportunity to people watch. The one little town bar offered another people-watching opportunity. Whatever it was that drew thousands to this little burg, she didn't know, but they didn't lack for entertainment when they got here.

The bar offered a better opportunity for finding an eligible bachelor to keep her out all night and do something wild and crazy with a sexy stranger. Women did that. It wasn't that pathetic. Or maybe it was, but since Marc hadn't shown up, she deserved to do something pathetic.

She'd managed to turn him off in one night. Must be the whiff of Eau d'Desperation she kept wearing. It was possible that he had something or someone else to do tonight, but Paul and Ida both seemed really surprised that he hadn't been in. Angela had been so sure Marc would return tonight that she'd volunteered to take Alex to the mall for shoes.

What if it was something she'd done last night? She'd been as attentive as possible in the context. That's what men liked. A woman who would hang on their every word. Now she was an attentive woman in four-inch heels and a short skirt, but Marc hadn't shown up. Though, most of her married customers had. Obviously, she could only attract married men. Tomorrow, despite the damage to her tips, it was a burqa. One of those blue ones like the women in Afghanistan wore with the netting over the eyes. That way she wouldn't be responsible for any marital spats.

Alex took off the dratted shoes and carried them into the kitchen.

"Give up on them shoes?" Frankie asked.

"They're hard to mop in." She set the shoes on her purse. Both pinky toes were angry red and puffy to the point of being shiny, and she couldn't even go home and soak them. Today was working out to be spectacular. Rejected. Looking stupid for wearing a short skirt and heels to wait tables and bearing the guilt of dozens of men, and at least one woman, who had lust in their hearts for her when they were supposed to be in committed long-term relationships with significant others, kids, and an SUV. There was a special place in hell for people like her.

Alex Perkins, the Typhoid Mary of marriage. Ruining unions left and right, but immune to Mr. Right herself.

The bell on the door jingled, reminding Alex that she hadn't locked up, so she hurried out to the dining room before whoever it was seated themselves and decided what they wanted. "I'm sorry, we're closed."

"That's okay. I'm pretty sure Ida won't mind if I hang out until you're finished." Marc, in expensive jeans and another concert T-shirt, grinned at her.

Now he showed up. When her feet were the size of watermelons, her short skirt spotted with grease, ketchup, and who knew what else, and her makeup half worn off.

"I don't know about that," she told him.

"I do."

Frankie came out carrying a bottlebrush. Great choice of weapons. Good thing they weren't being held up. "Oh, hi, Marc. You want something to drink?"

"Nah. I'm good. How are you doing, Frankie?"

"Dishwasher's broken. I gotta wash everything by hand."

Marc glanced at Alex and then smiled at Frankie. "Let me take a look at it. In another life I used to do some repair work, and I'm not doing anything until Alex is ready to go."

What the—? Never mind. She didn't want to know. She stacked the plates from the last table and handed them to Marc on his way past. After all he'd put her through today, even if he didn't know it, he might as well be useful.

Before she could mop the floor, she had to finish wiping the tables and put up the chairs. Marc's arrival must mean that he was interested, now that she'd made a firm decision about her life. Firmish, at least. She wrung out her cloth. Damn, what to do?

She could walk away from this train wreck and go back home to lick her wounds, soak her feet, and consider joining a nunnery. She'd have to convert to Catholicism and there was probably a waiting period, but it would be worth it. Married to God, she'd never have to risk a broken heart. Oh, wait, she couldn't go home because Finn and Angela were making babies.

Or she could stick to the plan, be his ideal woman, and play dumb about his fame. Not entirely fair to him, though. Pretending to be the girl of his dreams. She would be trading the guilt of being the Other Woman for the guilt of being a fake gold digger. Not the greatest solution, but this wasn't a life-long relationship, and it could be a good learning experience.

Nope, that wasn't sitting super well either.

What she needed was to go *home* home, but that entailed dealing with the parents who wanted to know all about the boyfriend she'd dated for five years, never brought home, and broken up with before they met him. *Hello, Mom and Dad. I'd like you to meet Roger, and here are pictures of Roger's wife and son and new baby. Yeah, I'm a home wrecker. Aren't you proud?* She needed to put in a call to the university library to see if they could use a little help over the summer again. Go back to the dorm. Wallow there in comfort and safety while dodging Roger. Maybe use her tips to get a nice hair shirt to wear for additional penance.

She'd only broken it off with Roger a couple months ago. She wasn't ready for a relationship. It wasn't fair to Marc to hoodwink him either.

Dumping the mop bucket, she said, "Hey Frankie, I'm headed out."

"Yeah, yeah. See you tomorrow." Frankie waved her off, consumed by the sight of the dishwasher gurgling away in front of him.

Marc frowned. "Where are you going?"

Alex held up her pointer fingers. "I'm finished cleaning up, so I'm leaving." Using both hands, she pointed over her shoulders for emphasis. Just in case he didn't get it.

His shirt was damp and sticking to an impressive six-pack. Sweet little sixteen would have been gaga. Not-so-sweet twenty-three was just a little tingly at the sight. Kind of the same reaction a hot guy on TV would get. Except that not-so-sweet twenty-three couldn't stop staring, but was intent on charting denial.

It didn't matter what either of them thought. Her walking away now was the best thing for everyone. Safer by far.

"Can't you wait a few minutes? We're testing it, and then I can go."

"Since when did my leaving become contingent on your leaving?"

Marc blinked at her, frowning. "I thought I'd walk you home."

"Did you now? How quaint of you. But I'm not going home so the point is moot." She started to slide one foot into her shoe, but her screaming toe had to have been heard in North Carolina, so she stuffed the shoes into her heavy purse. The way things had been going, she'd step on glass in the dark and end up on crutches for the rest of the season.

"You have a date or something?"

"Alex? Have a date?" Frankie snorted. "Right."

Alex glared at him. Stupid kid.

The dishwasher hissed to a stop, and Frankie lost interest in her love life in favor of the steam-belching machine. He pulled out one glass and inspected it in the light as he tossed it from one hand to the other to keep from burning himself. "Awesome, Marc. I'm gonna get out of here before dawn."

Alex scanned the heaps of dirty dishes stacked on every available surface and doubted it. Then she turned and walked out of the kitchen. "You better lock this door after me," she called over her shoulder.

"Hey, don't run away." Marc followed her through the serving area and Frankie came behind him.

"This is not running. Running is defined as something faster than this. I believe, technically, I should have a longer stride, and at certain points, both feet are off the ground." Alex pushed through the door. If her stride got any longer, it could be defined as running. Whatever it was about this guy, she either wanted to run straight into his arms or far, far away.

"Okay then, walking real fucking fast." He slid out the door behind her and stopped while she waited for Frankie to lock up. "Is there something about me you don't like?"

Alex started to draw a breath and stopped. Yeah, there was something. It really was time to find the source of denial, and the source was Roger. Roger had pursued her. All the way through British Writers, Early and Modern. Two semesters he had courted her before she allowed herself to be captured. Before she finally bought the stories about how his wife didn't understand him and how he was leaving her and so on and so forth.

She wasn't running, or more accurately, hurrying away from Marc, but she *was* trying to get away from Roger, to prove that he could survive the summer, the rest of his life even, without her. Which was why she was in Potterville waiting tables and not working at the university library this summer. However, past experience did not always predict future results, and she knew for sure that this guy had an ex-wife, meaning he didn't have a current wife. Most likely.

If this thing with Marc went somewhere, she might fall in love with him and he might hurt her.

But he might not. It would be nice not to be alone. Nice to be able go out in public with the man she was dating. Nice to have him pay for dinner. Nice to try a little peach eating of her own for once instead of just reading about it. Supposing, of course, that he wasn't married. Because that was going to be a deal breaker. "You're not married, are you?"

"Hell, no. I just earned my six year chip for abstaining from that institution."

Alex finished the deep breath she'd been trying to draw earlier. He could be lying, but she'd asked. If he didn't tell the truth, she couldn't be blamed for his actions, or so she had been told. Hopefully. At least her profiling research this morning and last night wouldn't go to waste. And the town wanted it. "I was headed for some ice cream. You interested?"

"I am." He grinned.

Chapter 2

Interested? Shit, he'd traded interested for burning desire when he'd caught sight of her mopping the floor. This woman made cleaning sexy. That long lean body and cap of black hair. Eyes like diamond drill bits. A mouth that went from lush to sarcastic in twenty seconds flat.

And so smart. So smart. She had a comeback for everything. He'd gotten so used to phoning it in with everybody around him except Sandy and Suzi, that finding somebody who could do a little verbal smack down was almost better than finding a hot chick hiding in Potterville. Cassie was never, ever going to let him live this down. If she found out.

"So, ice cream?" he asked.

"Perfect weather for it."

"You don't live in Potterville, do you? I've never seen you here before." Marc fell into step beside her.

Alex frowned at him. They all seemed to think she was perfect for him, but she acted like he was barely worthy of consideration. "No, my cousin Angela said I could make a lot of money waiting tables over the summer, and I had driving reasons to get away from the university for a few months. Didn't we have this conversation already?"

Shit, yes they had. No wonder she was looking at him like he was losing IQ points with every step. "Yeah, I was just trying to refresh on the details. So you're in college."

"Hence the need for money."

"For school." Interesting. Most of the college students he'd run into had been groupies buying time, letting Mommy and Daddy pay for school until they had to get a job. If her folks were paying for school, she wouldn't need to be waiting tables to earn money. The expression on her face reminded him that his last comment was a shade on the stupid side. "I was just trying to figure out how old you are. So you're in college. What are you…" Damn, what was that question college kids always asked? He hadn't been to a uni party in decades. Too busy building a career. "What are you majoring in?"

"I'm working on a master's in Brit Lit. What about you? Are you in school?"

"No, I—" What was he supposed to say? *No, I'm a professional rock star, and I'm nearly twice your age. Besides, I always thought college was a waste of time and money reserved for snotty rich kids who didn't need to work for a living.* That would get her in bed. "I didn't go to college." Dear God, had he just admitted the truth?

"You didn't?"

And now she was looking at him like a stranger from a strange land. "I went to work straight out of high school." Bands through high school. Local guitar god by nineteen. Touchstone at twenty. Touring the world before his twenty-second birthday. Now at thirty-eight, he was a member of one of the top ten selling bands in history. It wasn't like he was a total loser.

"What do you do?"

Damn it. Now he had to tell her, and she was going to go all gaga and that would be the end of any hope of…of anything real. Might as well get it over with. "I'm a musician. I play guitar for Touchstone."

"Oh."

Oh? *Oh?* She must live in a box in a cave under a bridge. "You sound like you don't know who Touchstone is."

"I know who Touchstone is in *A Midsummer Night's Dream,* and I know there's a popular band by that name, but beyond that no. I don't follow modern music at all."

Huh. Marc had thought there were only two or three people left in the world who didn't know Touchstone, and one of them had married his drummer, so she knew now. Ida and Paul's matchmaking was much better than he'd assumed. They hadn't chucked the first attractive female who might suit; they had lined up a good candidate who didn't have any predisposed ideas. Since Dez, every woman he'd gone out with had been in it for the fame and money and not him. Alex gave him a chance to find out what she thought of him without her basing any preconceptions on his branding. Awesome. "What kind of ice cream do you want?"

"Strawberry. I like the classics." She grinned and it was bewitching. The curve of her mouth, the sparkle in her eyes. If the classics looked like her, he had been missing out in pursuit of the next big thing.

* * * *

Marc handed her the ice cream cone. The shop on the town square was swarming with people. Because of the late hour, it was mostly young couples, and several of them had stopped Marc for autographs and selfies on his way to and from the service window. He must be more famous than she'd thought.

"How is it?" Marc asked.

"Good. They make their own. Ida swears they pick all the fruit locally."

"I know. Cassie said this is their second year open. Since Jason built that house on the mountain, tourism has picked up, and the town was doing pretty steady business before then. The city council was approached by Coldstone and Baskin Robbins franchises, but they turned them down in favor of this family owned place. It's a better fit for the town brand."

Sales numbers, units, and business plans. Was that coffee ice cream or butter pecan he had? According to the all-knowing Internet, people who liked coffee ice cream were passionate and over-committed. Butter pecan meant he was sensitive, but wouldn't reveal himself to others. Was he fun and flirtatious or cautious and traditional? How was she supposed to know what to say if she didn't know what kind of person he was? "The whole town seems to be very invested in their image. My cousin calls it Mayberry-ness."

"Yeah, so does Cassie." Marc scanned the square. He must be bored. Or he was looking for a good place to sit. Did he like to people watch as much as she did?

It wasn't that he was a bad guy. Marc was extremely good looking. He just couldn't quote Keats or smile at her like she was the most clever, exciting woman in the world. Or maybe he could if she gave him a chance. "So tell me about yourself."

"There's not much that hasn't been in the press." He turned toward a bench beside the now empty bandstand. It was dim there, but not dark. The perfect balance of being well lit without being in a spotlight. So he didn't want to attract attention right now. Was that because he wanted to focus on her, or because he was tired of being mobbed by his many fans? Or did he not want to be seen with her? That wouldn't be a first. He settled onto the bench and turned toward her. "Tell you about myself."

What man didn't want to talk about himself? His Wiki page had not been forthcoming on his pet cause or even what kind of movies he liked. Liking sports just proved he was a regular man. It didn't supply her with any material. Alex sat down trying to mirror his pose, but when he crossed his ankle over his knee she gave up. There was no way to make that look good in this short of a skirt. "Just searching for a topic of conversation."

"Okay. What do you want to know?"

"Where do you stand on global warming or the deficit or Arab Spring?"

"Ah, well, I recycle, pay my taxes, and Arab Spring is making it difficult to get to Egypt, but I'm not certain what they're fighting about. What about you?"

Good question. "The same, I guess. Except I wasn't planning on going to Egypt any time soon." If he had an interest in Egypt, that was something she could study up on.

"Where were you planning to go?"

"Italy."

"What's in Italy?"

What's in Italy? He couldn't be that dumb, unless he was asking what she wanted to see. A test then.

"I mean, for you."

The Keats-Shelley Museum. Keats's grave. Trevi Fountain. The Sistine Chapel. Florence. Venice. The food. "The food. I love Italian food."

He nodded like that wasn't an odd, dopey thing to say. "Italy is nice. I've been there a couple of times on tour."

"What have you seen?"

"In Italy? The Vatican, a couple of the museums. The usual stuff, I guess." He shrugged. "I was focused on work at the time. It might be nice to go and just be on vacation." He stared into her eyes like he'd just asked a very important question.

Her breath caught in her throat, but was it excitement or panic? If he was implying that he wanted to go to Italy with her, it could be either. She'd been pleased when he wanted to sit in the square eating ice cream like a publicly acceptable couple on a regular date. Alex arched a little more to enhance her assets and quell her nervous stomach.

"Listen, I know that Paul and Ida are up to something and if you're not interested, it's cool," Marc said.

"Paul and Ida are up to something?" Alex clenched her free hand into a fist. She hadn't assumed a fix-up was in progress until after work last night when Angela was so excited. He must have figured it out before she did, and he was okay with it. It would be awfully nice to come clean.

Nice and terrifying.

"Matchmaking. Didn't you know?"

Nope, not ready to be honest yet. Not the absolute truth. "No, but it fits. My cousin was very interested that we met."

Marc draped his arm across the back of the bench so that his fingertips just brushed her sleeve. "I'm not surprised if Angela is in on it, too. Regardless, I don't want you to feel pressured."

Other than the tension in her chest that kept her from breathing properly, no pressure. "Not really. Nervous as hell, but not pressured."

He cocked his head. "Why nervous?"

"Because my taste in men is suspect." Gah, hadn't she just told herself she wasn't ready for the truth? It was too soon.

"Fair enough. My taste in women is suspect enough that my friends felt the need to fix me up with you." He shifted and the tips of his fingers brushed against her skin. Since she wasn't electrocuted on the spot, she decided she liked the sensation.

She shifted closer. Half an inch, but enough to get decent contact. He kept his gaze fixed on hers without moving. His fingers were calloused at the tips. The sensation of the calluses scraping across her skin ever so slightly with his pulse made it even harder to breath. No wonder he was famous. She was about to hyperventilate and pass out just from the tips of three of his fingers brushing her shoulder.

"Still nervous?"

"Little bit. You?" She started to see spots as her anoxia set in.

His lips curled. "Terrified."

* * * *

Marc glanced at the living room clock. Twelve o'clock. He could go get Alex. They had sat in the town square talking until midnight. She was great. Just amazing. Fun to talk to. The best part was that all they did was talk. When the town hall clock started chiming midnight, she swore and said she had to be up early to open at the diner. He had walked her back to her cousin's Craftsman style bungalow where she went up onto the porch, gave him a little wave, and let herself in. No skipping the introductions to suck face like most of the other women he'd met. No implying that he should take her home as soon as possible and give her the lifestyle she had always wanted to become accustomed to. What was important to her was her job and the commitments she'd made. She hadn't talked much about school, but that had to be important, too. She was getting a master's degree. People didn't do that without good reason. She'd left him wanting more, and since midnight, that want had been building.

He put aside his e-reader. Suzi's latest book had appeared in his e-mail this morning right before a message from Brian crowing that the new book was out. It was certainly putting him in the right mindset to see more of Alex. As he tied his shoes, his phone rang. He had to limp over to the table one shoe on and one shoe off, which reminded him of Alex's bare feet last night.

"Yeah?"

"You get my e-mail?" Jason demanded.

"E-mail? I haven't been online since first thing this morning."

"First thing? What time did you get up? It's only nine."

Marc pinched the bridge of his nose. He wasn't in the right frame of mind to deal with Jason. The man owned houses on both coasts and never took time zones into account. "No, what is it about?"

"I came up with a new riff last night. Woke up with it running around my head."

Super.

"I recorded it on the computer and sent it to you, but I've been thinking about it since I sent it, and I've got more. You want me to send you that, too?"

Marc checked at the clock. He was supposed to be driving down the mountain to see Alex, not listening to Jason be brilliant. But in the twenty-five years he'd known Jason, the other man hadn't matured more than a few minutes, so brushing him off wasn't going to work. "Hold on and let me pull up what you've already got." Marc glanced at the clock again. Alex awaited.

But Jason would not be put off.

"What do you think of the house?" Jason asked as Marc fiddled open his laptop and got it started.

"It's great."

"I told you you'd like it."

"You didn't tell me half the town would be intent on fixing me up with a waitress at Ida's."

"Jeez, you should have known. It's Potterville."

"Okay, shut up a minute." Marc clicked play.

The riff was simple and perfect, unbelievable that no one had ever done it before, but it didn't sound like anything he'd ever heard.

"What do you think?" Jason demanded as the last note faded away.

Shithead. Woke up in the middle of the night with a brilliant riff and by morning had dreamed up a completely brilliant melody. "Absolutely, man. What do you have for lyrics?"

"Eh, scrambled eggs."

Marc forced a laugh. Funny he should reference the original lyrics to The Beatles' "Yesterday" when he might have just come up with another song of that caliber. In his sleep. Bastard.

"I sent the riff to Ty, but I think he's sleeping off last night, and Brian's reading a book."

The way Jason said Brian was reading a book made it sound like Brian had taken up taxidermy and was building a squirrel army in his basement. Of course, as crazy as Brian was about Suzi's books, he wouldn't surface again until he'd read it twice and had a long girly chat with Suzi. He wasn't going to be writing lyrics for a while, and if somebody didn't shepherd Jason through the rest of this song right now, it was going to be gone.

Alex would have to wait. Business had to come first. She'd understand.

"Let me grab a guitar so I can noodle along."

Goddamn it.

* * * *

Alex checked the time again. Last night, on the sidewalk in front of Angela and Finn's house, he had said he would meet her here today so they could go do something after her shift. She'd worn flats to work and stuffed the heels in her purse. She'd brought makeup to put on. If she could have stuffed a shower and a change of clothes in her bag, she would have. For him. And he didn't show.

Probably for the best. It was too soon after Roger for her to get into any kind of relationship.

Even a perfect relationship with a gorgeous man who seemed to like her. At least she hadn't told anyone he was coming today. See, it was subconscious. She'd known it wasn't going to happen, so she'd kept it quiet to keep from being embarrassed when he dumped her. Not dumped, but lost interest after one date.

Alex delivered meals to tables, took orders, placed them with the kitchen, refilled drinks, watched the door, checked the clock.

God, why didn't he come? He had seemed so interested last night.

She hadn't kissed him goodnight. She should have at least given him a peck on the cheek.

Alex's stomach knotted and she licked her lips. A good-night kiss was de rigueur, and it wasn't like she hadn't been wondering what his lips would taste like.

It was for the best. She needed to get her head on straight after Roger. He was still going to be her academic advisor next year, and she needed to be able to work with him while not falling into old patterns. She'd come too far to not get her thesis approved.

Marc might have a reason for not coming. Something could have happened to his family or one of his friends. He might have sent a text letting her know that he was running behind or that he was going to meet her someplace later. All her tables were fine for the moment so she darted to the back and grabbed her purse before ducking into a bathroom stall.

No messages.

Alex sunk down on the toilet and covered her face with her hands. Not only was she Typhoid Mary, spreading marital distress and immune to Mr. Right, she was immune to all single men.

This was so pathetic and melodramatic it was Byronic. She was an Eliot scholar. Alex pulled herself up and brushed her hands through her hair. Right now, the best thing for her was to be single and learn to do that well. Which meant leaving the bathroom and facing people. No problem. Before she left, she checked herself in the mirror. Calm exterior. No odd coloration or facial tics. The picture perfect waitress who was not having a nervous breakdown.

"Alex, where have you been?" Ida was in the kitchen when she came through from dropping her purse in her locker. Very bad sign. Ida never came in the kitchen. She ran the dining room and left the kitchen to Paul. "You have three new tables and they all look like they're ready to order."

"Stop it, you old bat. Leave her alone." Paul banged a plate into the serving window. Paul was scowling at the food. Also a bad sign.

Ida stared at Paul for a beat and then turned to Alex, her frown melting as she did. "All right, sweetie, can you hurry on out and take care of those tables?"

Okay, so maybe the nervous breakdown was visible. "I just had to go to the bathroom. I washed my hands." Alex held up her hands, which reminded her that she had not, in fact, washed when she was in the bathroom.

"You know the rule," Paul said, giving her uncharacteristic doe eyes. "You wash in my sink before you handle my food."

Ida nodded, pouching out her lip and, dear Lord, blinking back tears.

They were both acting more like critical care nurses than the drill sergeants they were. She should ask what the hell was going on, but the answer wasn't going to benefit her, so she went to wash her hands in the kitchen sink before heading out to the dining room. Every time Ida came near, she patted Alex's arm. Paul didn't even snarl when she dropped a plate on the floor, requiring him to remake the meal. Tina and Drew kept looking at her funny every time she bumped into them. How miserable.

As soon as her shift was over, she ran back to Angela's house, changed into her dowdiest clothes, left her phone behind, and made it back to the square just in time to catch the World War II tour to Dolly Sods.

Surrounded by tourists who didn't know anything about her sordid past or her recent mess, she wouldn't have to think about any of it. Just her and rocks and wildflowers and the occasional mortar shell.

* * * *

"You," Ida snarled. The customer who had been in the middle of paying his bill flinched. "No, not you. Him." Ida pointed one of her long, and today neon green, fingernails at Marc. Sorta like being nailed to the wall.

"What did I do?" Getting a working demo of a new song was always a high, but the high was wearing off fast. First, Alex wasn't at her house or answering her phone. Then, Angela and Finn didn't know why Alex wasn't home, where she went, or why she wouldn't be answering her phone. Now, the attitude from Ida. Awesome.

"Where have you been?"

The customer shoved his money across the counter and hurried out. Every other diner appeared to take this as the floorshow. Super awesome.

"I was working. Do you know where Alex is?"

"Probably at home crying her eyes out." Ida slammed the cash drawer closed, hard enough to push the whole thing within millimeters of the edge of the counter.

"I tried there, but she wasn't home."

"Are you sure?" Ida planted her fists on her hips. "Maybe she just didn't want to open the door to you."

"It's a possibility. I didn't go around peeking in the windows." Though when he stopped at Finn's office to inquire, Angela had offered him the keys, so he could have checked the closets if he'd wanted. "Why? Was she upset when she left here?"

"You!"

Marc spun around. Paul was standing in the kitchen doorway pointing a carving fork at him. "How could you?"

"Paul, we been through this. Weren't you listening?" Ida snapped.

"I just saw he was here. What did I miss?" Paul lowered the fork.

"This is better than the soaps," one of the women in the booth behind Marc said to her friend.

"Wait a minute." Marc put up a hand. It was bad enough having his personal life discussed on the Internet. He had no desire to become dinner theater, too. He headed for the kitchen, and both Ida and Paul followed him. No one in the dining room moved except a couple of little kids who munched on fries and chicken tenders as they watched. "Okay, was Alex upset that I didn't show up today?"

Paul and Ida glanced at each other. Ida, consummate performer that she was, had framed herself in the service window so the audience could still enjoy their private conversation. Paul, Marc noticed, had not gotten into frame, and by the look on his face, it was only because he was so flustered. Crap. Alex was mad and, if he guessed right, she was the icy quiet type who could reduce a man to splinters with a well-phrased remark. If he'd told Jason to hang on long enough to send her a text to let her know he was going to be late, all this could have been averted.

"Well, not as much as you'd notice," Ida said. "But we know her, and she was broken up."

Drew leaned in from the side door. "What's going on?"

"Drew, was Alex upset before she left?" Marc asked.

"Not weepy upset. She looked pissed to me, and she just kept getting more and more pissed." Drew rolled his eyes. "Especially when she dropped that plate, and you didn't say anything."

"It was an accident," Paul said. "I understood."

"Just like you always do."

"Boys!" Ida glared at them. "This is beside the point. Marc, you stood Alex up and that is just unacceptable."

"I didn't stand her up."

"You weren't supposed to meet her here today after her shift?" Paul asked. "Why? She's perfect for you."

"I said I would try, but I didn't make any promises." He had woken up early this morning smiling because he was going to see her. He would have been pacing around waiting until it was time to go if he hadn't had a good book to read. He might have even left early to pick her up.

He needed to call Suzi and tell her she was screwing up his love life.

"Last night we just left it at maybe."

"But she is perfect for you," Paul wailed.

"Will you stop saying that?" Marc rubbed his forehead. "Did it ever occur to you that she's not into me?"

"No," Drew said. Ida and Paul both turned on him. He looked at both of them for a second before ducking outside.

"Now, Marc, why wouldn't she be sweet on you?" Ida patted his arm.

"Don't you think if she was, she'd be someplace I could find her? I was only a little late."

"Two hours past her shift." Ida glanced through the service window at the sound of the front door bell and hurried out to deal with the new customers.

"Why don't you ask Angela where she went?" Paul asked.

"I already did. She doesn't know." Marc shrugged. Somewhere out there Alex was either suicidal that he'd stood her up or plotting his murder. His gut lurched. Damn it, a girl he liked, who wasn't into him for his money or connections, and he'd whiffed it by assuming she'd run on his schedule like the self-centered bastard he was. "It's okay. Doesn't matter. I'll send her a text. She doesn't have to answer it." Easy out for her. Less painful for both.

"Marc, don't give up so easily," Paul said.

"Order up!" Drew shouted from the side door. "Oh, sorry, I didn't know you were still in here. Order up, Paul."

Business resumed as usual before Marc had made it to the front door. Last night she'd seemed perfect, but this disappearing act either meant she didn't like him or she was playing hard to get. If she didn't like him, fine, lots of other people did. If she was playing games, he didn't like her. Nothing turned him off faster than a game player. Dez spent most of their relationship making him prove how much he loved her, and that was never going to happen again. Marc stopped at the driver's side door to check the street. People wandered around town like any other day. Blue skies and sunshine. He climbed in to head back up the mountain.

At Jason's house, Marc listened to the new demo again. It was good. Really good.

Good enough to have lost Alex because he was too busy working to meet her?

Work came first. Work always came first. Nobody got to the top without making a few sacrifices. Plus, if Alex was one of those high maintenance chicks who couldn't take a little delay then she wasn't going to be able to deal with his life. Suzi said being in a relationship with a rock star was like being trapped in a doctor's office trying to get your seven minutes.

Suzi. If he hadn't been reading her goddamn book, he would have left early and not gotten sucked into working with Jason.

Snatching up his phone, he called her.

"Hello?"

"You are ruining my life."

"I'm sorry. How am I managing that from this distance?" Something clicked on her end. It sounded like her laptop. Suzi was never far from it and she must have closed it. Hopefully that was the case. Then she'd be listening.

"I was reading your book and was late to meet someone."

"So you like it?"

"Of course I like it, but it ruined my life."

"This person didn't wait when you were a few minutes late, or was my book so gripping that you totally lost track of time and were hours late? This is very important for marketing purposes."

Marc inspected his fingernails. Alex had seemed to like him last night. Why hadn't she waited? Okay, two hours was pretty late, but she hadn't tried to text him either. "I was two hours late."

"Really? I'm flattered. Can I use that quote on my website?"

Marc rolled his eyes. "Sure."

Her computer opened. "So what's her name?"

"Alex. How did you know it was a woman?"

"If it was a man, you'd have called Bear." Keys clicked. In seconds, half the planet was going to think he'd been so engrossed in her book that he'd been two hours late for a date. Good for her sales at least. "So tell me about her."

"She's okay I guess."

"Right. Which explains you calling me to whine. Did you try calling her?"

"No answer." Marc stretched out on the couch. It gave him a good vantage to study Cassie's infamous shotgun over the fireplace. It must be nice to have someone love you that much. He'd been under the impression that Dez did, but she had just been very good at playing her games.

"Text?" The computer closed again. Once more he had her undivided attention.

"Yeah. I was hoping it would be non-committal. If she's not interested, she doesn't have to respond."

"I need a backtrack. When did you meet her?"

"Couple of days ago at the diner."

"Oh, Alex the waitress, right?"

"How do you know?"

"Cassie told me that Ida said she had a waitress working this summer who she thought would be good for you. Witty, tall, skinny, dark hair, some deep dark secret in her recent past." Suzi sipped something. "You know, if she has recent baggage you're going to have to work a little harder. That is, if you really want her."

I do. "Maybe. What are you thinking?"

"Without knowing what the deep, dark baggage is, I'd say just remain available and laid back. Kind of like you're trying to coax a deer to eat out of your hand. It's not going to be easy. This woman is not going to throw herself at you."

A deer? Great. The last time he'd been patient with a woman it had ended in divorce. But Alex wasn't Dez. "Okay, so I screwed up today and didn't meet her like I was supposed to, but I called and I texted. What's the next big move?"

"If it was my story, I'd have the hero arrange to bump into her so he could explain his boorish behavior and open up the possibility of another meeting. She's working at the diner. Are you going to be hungry tomorrow?"

"Oh, God, I forgot you were writing romances now, too."

"I don't tell you about those. They sell well."

"Better than the horror?"

"Hands down."

"So I need to 'bump into' Alex tomorrow and explain why I was late."

"Feel free to tell her you were reading a fantastic new book by Suzette Miranda Bazian. Say it really loud so neighboring diners can hear."

"I'll be sure to do that. Thanks."

"If I'm going to ruin your life, I should attempt to fix it." Suzi coughed. "Um, before you go, do you know a groupie named Gillian Rosetti?"

"I don't know. Why?"

"She's been following Savitar this tour. Logan says he won't do anything with her or with any of them, but this Gillian girl has been really aggressive. She scares me a little."

"I don't know what to tell you, Suz. Groupies are a job hazard. You're either going to have to learn to accept groupies or get him into a TV show to keep him occupied. We did *House* last tour. It kept us busy and out of trouble except for Ty deciding he was dying every other day."

"Okay. I'll try."

"If you're bored, you can come here to Jason's and help me fix the problem you caused."

"That would go over great. 'Hi, I'm Suzi. I'm here to facilitate you falling in love with Marc. Let me tell you the features and drawbacks of being with a rock star.'"

"On second thought."

She was so fun. Why couldn't he find a girl just like Suzi?

"I knew it. Good luck with your girl. Remember, coaxing a deer to eat out of your hand."

"Great. You know how patient I am." He hung up the phone. Shoot, he should have asked Suzi what the difference was between a woman being nervous and a woman playing games.

Chapter 3

Alex rolled over. She'd slept as much as she could stand. Eventually, she had to face a world that thought she should be destroyed over the loss of a man. A man she never had in the first place. A man she wasn't sure she wanted or deserved in the first place. Sure, he was good looking, well built, intelligent, fun to be around.

Angela peeked through the sliver of the door that she'd opened with an exaggerated pout. "I'm so sorry."

Ah, yes, this was why she'd come back from Dolly Sods and set off on the next bus for the stargazing trip in a different part of the park. To avoid Angela's unwarranted pity. Angela, who should have been at the office by now. Alex glanced at her alarm clock. Ten-thirty. Yup, Angela should have been at long gone. "About what?"

"Marc. I heard he stood you up yesterday." She pushed the door open the rest of the way and the scent of bacon and eggs wafted through the door. "I thought I would make you breakfast."

Alex's stomach clenched. "I'm not hungry."

"I'm sure. Can you try to eat something?"

Nausea rolled up her throat into her nose with a buzzing sensation. Maybe these were the symptoms she had from her weird matrimonial illness. She'd never been one of those girls who planned and re-planned their marriage from the age of six, but here she was, somehow buying into the belief that she wasn't a valid human unless she was married and every relationship had to have that as its logical end. Not every pair bond ended up married. Sometimes they married and it ended badly. Sometimes they just had fun for a while and drifted apart.

Sometimes they chose to live in some weird state of celibacy while trying to match up everyone within sight.

Dear God, she was going to end up like Ida and Paul.

Alex threw off the covers. "Suddenly, I'm starved."

Within one egg and half a sausage, Alex was back to fighting with herself about whether she'd done something to turn Marc off, and if she wanted him, or any man, in her life right now.

"I need to be finishing up my thesis and getting into a doctoral program." She shook her fork to bring the point home. "That's what's important."

"Is that what you plan to do? Get a doctorate? I thought you wanted to work for a magazine."

Alex opened her mouth, but nothing came out. Here she was sitting at a table in her cousin's house wondering what she planned to do with her life. High school summer vacations all over again. "Well, that was a long time ago. Things change."

"I remember when we were kids, we used to put together our own magazine when you came to visit Gramma and Papaw in the summers." Angela poured her a big glass of orange juice. "Davey Wegman used to draw all the pictures for us, and you wrote the articles, and I sold advertising."

"Sold? I seem to remember trading Lou at the diner for cookies and Ben at the post office for rides around town in the post office truck."

"I convinced Miss Hall to let us use the library copier to print our magazine."

"Where is Davey now?"

"He's an art teacher in Cincinnati."

"Oh, good. He was an excellent artist."

"So what changed your mind about working at a magazine?"

Roger. Roger changed her mind. In British Writers, Early and Modern. "I don't know. Just changed my mind."

"But you could still go work for a magazine."

Alex shrugged. "I guess." Ugh, school. One year to finish the master's, two for the doctorate to spend the rest of her life teaching British Writers, Modern and Early. Publish or perish. Reliving her own mistakes every single semester in an endless loop.

"You just don't seem very happy about going to school anymore."

"I guess I'm not, but I'm almost done."

"But you're not sure anymore. You broke up with your boyfriend, and now you don't know. Maybe you should give Marc another chance. Did you look at your phone to see if he tried to call? He might have had a good excuse yesterday."

And there it was. The entire reason Angela stayed home and cooked breakfast. After all, Angela had given Finn dozens and dozens of chances he didn't even know he'd gotten.

"It's not a big deal."

"Sure it is. I saw you yesterday morning. You were happy when you thought he liked you. Did you look at your phone?"

Her phone was buried in her purse under five pounds of yesterday's tips that she hadn't bothered to roll in her rush to get out of the house. But if he had tried to call or text, that would mean that he was interested and did care, which made her the type of woman who made a man prove over and over that he cared. Craptastic. "It doesn't matter."

"Why not? He came to the office and said you weren't home, and Ida said he showed up looking for you at the diner after you left."

The office? Finn's accounting office. Bet he loved that. Wait, Ida said? "Ida said?"

"She called me yesterday."

Of course she did. This whole town was wired for gossip. If terrorists ever made the mistake of setting up in Potterville, they'd be found out within a week and converted to Mom, apple pie, and baseball within two. Alex scooped the rest of her egg into her mouth. "I'm going to the library to work on my thesis before my shift."

"Why?"

"Because I'm this close, and I might as well finish." Alex stood up. She needed to be out of here right now.

"But you could work on it here just as well. All the research is on your computer." Angela followed her down the hall to the bathroom.

"But it's very quiet in the library and I can concentrate better." The library also made and ideal place to hide from Marc. He might turn up at Finn and Angela's house, but there was no way he'd show up at the library. Unless Angela told him where she was. Hmm, plot hole. Alex put toothpaste on her toothbrush, and then stared at herself in the mirror.

What if she had told Angela where she was going to be because she secretly wanted Marc to come find her but didn't want anyone, including herself, to think she was sitting at home waiting for him?

She should have gone for a psychology degree so she could sit around all day analyzing herself.

Alex rushed through her morning ablutions, scooped up her backpack, and ran for the door. "Thanks for breakfast. I won't be back until late. Good luck with you know what."

The library was not quiet. Not in a traditional library sense. It wasn't a library either. They loaned books, but only to residents. To the tourists, they seemed to have a running book sale that turned them into more of a bookstore. Alex had commented after her first trip there that she was surprised there wasn't a coffee shop inside. Angela hadn't gotten the reference, but Finn said it might be a profitable idea. Next summer there would probably be a homegrown version of Starbucks in the front corner between the checkout-slash-sales desk and the bathrooms.

Alex sequestered herself in one of the study carrels in the back corner and focused on her paper. She'd assembled all the research. Now it was a matter of organizing it, which should be the easy part, but it had been defeating her since March when Roger's wife gave birth.

Psychology. She should have majored in psychology. Right now she could be finishing up a master's thesis on how people screwed up their lives because of poor decisions regarding love.

No progress on her thesis was made by the time she needed to get work. Alex packed up her stuff and walked along the baking sidewalk to the diner. Junie Keyes was in the kitchen racing back and forth like the grill was on fire. Tina stood between a couple and a family who were arguing over a table stacked with dishes. The outside eating area wasn't open yet. No Ida. No Paul. Not even Drew.

"Oh, my God, I am so glad you are here!" Tina grabbed Alex's arms and shook her. "You didn't answer your phone."

No, because the phone was still at Angela's. "What happened?"

"Ida went to the hospital."

"When?"

"Half an hour ago."

"Paul went with her?"

"Yeah."

"And they left you in charge?" What the hell were they thinking? No emergency warranted leaving Tina in charge.

"Neither you or Drew was answering your phone."

Alex scanned the room. Four fuming tables, two with no menus, one shaking an upside down coffee cup, the last frowning at a bill. Two tables piled with dishes. Three other tables in various states of eating. Both benches out front full of people waiting, who were no doubt considering a run over the mountain to someplace where they could get food before they expired of hunger. "How bad is Ida?"

"She went in an ambulance."

So anything between a panic attack and a heart attack. "Hey, Junie, is your mom home?"

"My mom?"

No, Godzilla. "Yeah, your mom. Can she come in and help out? Lunch rush is imminent."

"I'll call her. Order up." Junie banged a plate on the service counter so hard it should have shattered.

The door jingled behind Alex. A mild looking man and a redheaded woman stood in front of the counter. Both of them looked vaguely familiar so they must be townies. Alex stepped forward to stop them before they got too far inside. "I'm sorry, but we don't have any tables open—"

"Mr. and Mrs. Geoffrey!" Tina threw her arms around the redheaded wife and started to sob.

"Oh, honey, it'll be okay." Mrs. Geoffrey patted her back. "How can we help?"

Mr. Geoffrey held out his hand. "You must be Alex. Paul called us from the hospital. We figured you might need us."

"Great. Can you clear those tables?" Alex pointed to the piled tables and hurried to the service window to figure out which order slip went with the food Junie had just put in the window. Seconds after she delivered it, the doorbell jingled again. The way that the Geoffrey's greeted them, they had to be locals. Alex headed for the coffee cup waver, and when she turned to deal with the bill-frowner, she found that Finn, who she hadn't even noticed arriving, was already on the case as Angela handed out menus and filled people in on specials. Junie's mother arrived and set to work in the kitchen. Through the window, Alex noticed that some enterprising townsperson had opened up the outside seating and had started putting people at tables there. One of the librarians arrived and went to work taking orders. A girl in ridiculous high heels and a two-hundred dollar haircut also started taking orders. More townspeople arrived to seat people outside and stopped to gossip with each other while hogging the coffee pot and forgetting to give people water. Meals stacked up in the service window. Diners started going in search of the coffee and refilling their own drinks. *Things fall apart, the center cannot hold. Mere anarchy is loosed on the world.* She was in the storage room hunting for flatware because everything in the dining room was dirty when she heard the cash register ring. Alex ran out to it.

"Thanks for coming," Finn said waving the customers out the door.

"What are you doing?" Alex demanded.

"They wanted to go so I rang them up. I know how to handle money. I'm an accountant."

John-John sat on Ida's stool munching on a cookie and staring at her. Alex did not want to know where he got that cookie, or why he was here in the first place.

Behind her, a plate smashed, hushing the steady chorus of "excuse me" from diners who had not yet gone freelance with their service.

Into that silence, the door opened and in stepped Marc.

So this was what drove Tina to throw herself into Mrs. Geoffrey's arms sobbing. Alex forced herself back a step just so she wouldn't drop into his embrace like a hysterical mess. Her jaw ached from the effort of not crying with relief.

"Something wrong?"

"Nothing we can't handle," Finn grumbled.

Alex decided she needed to find out what the history was there some other time. Right now, she had a super volcano rumbling right under her. She needed to get it under control before Paul called to find out how everything was going and had to be told the business had been destroyed in a few unattended minutes. "Ida went to the hospital. Paul went with her." Alex checked her watch, frowned, and squinted at it. A very few unattended minutes. "About an hour ago. And it's lunch rush early." She glanced out the window. Outside seating was full, but she wasn't sure how many were tourists and how many were loitering locals.

Marc smirked at her like they shared a joke. "You seem to have a little more help than you need."

Alex tapped her nose.

"Okay." He drew a deep breath, surveying the scene. "Finn, are you okay on the register?"

"I know how to run it if that's what you mean."

Marc leveled a serious glare at Finn. "I mean, can you do this for the rest of the afternoon because I don't know how, and Alex is going to be busy."

"Fine." Finn shrugged like he was doing Marc a favor.

"Alex, can you sort out the kitchen? I need somebody with some experience managing the traffic flow out of there."

"Okay." Alex had gotten to the service window before she realized how he'd charmed her into doing what he wanted. By the time she turned around, Marc had his arm around the girl with the ridiculous high heels and the expensive haircut and was working her. While Alex figured out which orders were duplicates and where the rest needed to go, the noise level in the dining room dropped to a normal clatter and hum.

Marc came up behind her, just enough in her peripheral vision that she didn't wallop him with a plate. "How's it going?"

"How did you do this?"

"Do what?"

Alex tipped her head toward the quiet, happy dining room.

"It wasn't anything. I'm just doing half of Ida's job. Finn's doing all the checks."

"It was chaos when you walked in."

"Everybody wanted to help. It was just a matter of directing them. I have some practice at that. A little flattery goes a long way, too."

He was very good at getting what he wanted. Here she was falling for another line. Her old friend nausea climbed up her throat. "Yes. I suppose it does. Hey, Kady, you have an order."

Jeanie, who had been about to put the plates in the window, flinched, and one of the plates in her hand slipped. Marc didn't move away, but he cocked his head like he was studying Alex. At least she wasn't the only one psychoanalyzing her.

"Thanks, Alex." Kady butted between them, forcing Marc back a step. "You know, this is fun. I spend all my days behind a desk talking to the same six people. It's nice to get out and talk to normal folks." She flashed them a big smile, grabbed her plates, and hurried back out to mix with her customers.

"Alex?" Marc murmured.

Fascinated, she watched him extend his hand to touch her arm and pause just as his fingers grazed her skin. Her breath caught in her throat at the sensation. *A little flattery goes a long way.* That was what he'd said. It sure did.

"Are you okay?"

"Fine. Orders are starting to stack up." Alex kept her gaze in the kitchen where no orders were appearing, but both Jeanie and her mother were trying to eavesdrop while appearing busy. Mom was better at it than Jeanie. Neither was getting anything useful done in the meantime.

Now Marc took a step back. "All right." He tapped the counter twice with his long fingers and walked away. Behind her, she could hear him chatting with customers and keeping things going.

"Are you crazy?" Jeanie hissed.

"Jeanie," her mother snapped.

"Mom, do you know who that is? He's gorgeous and he's rich and he's so nice. How can you be such a—" Jeanie's lips had pressed together to form the first phoneme of the next word before she remembered that her mother was next to her.

It was enough for her mother to swat Jeanie on the shoulder. "Watch your tongue."

"Can we just get some orders finished up here?" Alex flicked through the bills on the shelf. "We have hungry people, and we don't want to disappoint Ida and Paul."

Her arm still tingled from his very slight touch. Jeanie was right. She was crazy, and she was being a bitch. But another man who got whatever he wanted with a little flattery? This, she did not need unless she wanted to try the hair of the dog that bit her. She scanned the dining room so she could get a glimpse of him. He was standing beside a table chatting up the diners who were loving it. As charming as he was, he couldn't be as charismatic as Roger.

* * * *

Alex cleared her last table. Paul had shown up after three with the news that Ida was resting at home wearing a heart monitor, though they suspected she'd had a panic attack. Then he took over the kitchen. Once the drama was over, the townspeople drifted back to whatever they had been doing before the interruption, leaving only diners. After that, it was pretty much back to normal…with one exception.

Marc had stuck around all day hosting and being pleasant and confusing and leaving her no way to sneak out of there to think.

"Hey."

Alex jumped. One of the water glasses in her hand slipped and smashed on the concrete.

"Sorry, didn't mean to scare you." Marc crouched with her to help pick up the broken glass. "Crazy day, huh?

"You could say that. I'm glad Ida is okay."

"I'm not sure what this town would do without her." Marc lifted the plates out of her hands. "I came in here today to talk to you."

"Why?" Alex focused on dusting up the last retrievable shards with her cloth so she wouldn't have to look at him.

"Sorry I missed you yesterday. My buddy called with a new song. He wanted to finish it up right away. That's why I didn't call to let you know I was running late."

"Oh." Jeanie was right. She was being a bitch. "That's okay. I wanted to go to Dolly Sods after work anyway, and then I decided to go with the star-watching group. There are a lot more stars here than at home."

"I know what you mean."

She stood up and he followed suit.

"I sent you a text."

"Sorry. I forgot my phone at home." Intentionally.

"So are you busy tonight? It's early. We could still make the movie. Then ice cream after? I'm shooting for a do over." He smiled, so she returned it.

Ice cream the other night had just been getting-to-know-you, but the movie made it a date. He probably would have taken her to dinner first if they hadn't just spent all day working in a diner. Wow. A date. He wanted to go on a date, in public, with her. Very standard. A movie and ice cream. No pressure, but her stomach still wanted to cower around her spine. "Okay. I just have to finish up here."

"I'll get these to the kitchen while you wipe down the table. How's that?" He lifted the unharmed glass and the broken glass-filled towel out of her hands with just the lightest touch of his fingers.

"Thanks."

Chapter 4

The movie was the original *Frankenstein* with Boris Karloff. Marc draped his arm across the back of Alex's chair and sat with one ankle resting on the other knee, taking up as much space as he could. By the end of the movie, her butt was numb because she didn't know how to sit, but didn't want to move out of fear that he would think she was uncomfortable. That made no sense because she *was* uncomfortable. She was turning into Jane Eyre, riding backward in the carriage even though it made her sick because she didn't want to cause trouble. And what did that win Jane? Nothin'.

But then on the way to ice cream several people stopped them to get his autograph and take pictures. Of both of them. Together. Why they wanted pictures of her with him she didn't know, but he wasn't hiding the fact that they were together.

Refreshing. Maybe Jane had something with that backward carriage riding.

"Strawberry, right?"

"Please."

"Go ahead and find a place to sit."

Alex settled in the shadow of a tree. It wouldn't take more than five or ten minutes for him to get ice cream. Not enough time to sort out her thoughts. He was nice. He'd waded into the mess this morning without thinking twice and straightened it out like a master. Now, a real date. If he only wanted to get into her pants, he didn't have to do this much.

Not that she intended to jump into bed with any man who wandered by, but Marc could get female companionship much easier than all this. That implied that he wanted her, in particular. Which made no sense at all. Unless Paul and Ida had convinced him that she was the perfect woman.

She should have skipped Google and interrogated Ida and Paul.

"Here you go." Marc held out a strawberry ice cream cone.

Great, just in time to leave her with more questions than she'd started with.

"This is intimate."

Damn, she should have picked a brighter spot. "It seemed like it would be quiet."

"Yeah, sorry about the fans. They pay my living so I try to be nice to them."

"Good idea." The shadows were not helping her figure out whether he had coffee or butter pecan. "Good ice cream."

"It is."

"Ida says they make it right here and get all the produce locally." *And we had this conversation the day before yesterday.* "So tell me about this song."

"My buddy has a talent for coming up with good starts, but he's not strong on finishing things. He dreamed something up the other night and sent it to me, so I had to follow up before he lost interest." He licked his ice cream. "I miss the days before Garageband when Jason had to record what he'd come up with and mail it to me or come to my house in person. It gave me a little time between his genius brain farts."

"What's Garageband?"

"It's a computer program that lets you record right on the computer, and then you can attach the file to an e-mail. It's a nice program. Makes it easier for us to work together when we're not all in the same state. What about you? You said you were working on a master's degree on a writer?"

"Poet. Eliot. T. S. Eliot. I use Word."

"Word?"

"The word processing program." None of that made any sense at all. Her mouth was running and the *off* switch was stuck. She needed to fix that before she did too much damage.

"You'll have to introduce me to some Eliot. I'm always willing to learn." He grinned.

Or he could be into the idea. Alex leaned against the tree and crunched into her sugar cone. He didn't really want to know about Eliot, regret, and lost opportunity at a Victorian garden party. But this didn't feel like a line calibrated to get her into bed. He really wanted to get to know her, and unless she could invent some kind of bimbo character to protect her real identity fast, she was going to be herself.

"What did you think of the movie? Have you seen it before?"

And he tried again. Points for that. "I have, but it was a long time ago. It's nothing like the book."

"Really? How was the book different?"

"Lots of ways. Most importantly, the monster in the book was the doctor, not the creature."

"So the creature wasn't built of dead people?"

"Yes, but the creature had a good heart. Dr. Frankenstein was the bad guy. Kind of how the tool is not evil, but how it's used can be."

"Guns don't kill people, people kill people?"

"Yeah." Not a bad insight considering he hadn't read the book.

"Really? I might have to read it."

Maybe she could break out the poetry with him. Be a little more Jane Austen than Jane Eyre. "There's a movie version with Kenneth Branagh and Robert DeNiro that was very true to the original book."

"Maybe we could watch it together."

"Maybe." She scanned the square. The band concert was winding down and people were drifting away. On the far side, in front of the bank, stood a stocky man with dark hair. His face was in shadow because of the streetlight behind him, but he had to be staring at her.

Roger.

That bastard. He'd followed her. Well, he was going to get an eyeful.

"I love a man who's willing to learn." Alex chucked the remains of her ice cream cone on the grass, swung her leg over Marc's lap, and planted her lips on his. Butter pecan. One question answered. Not an important one, though, not straddled across him, enveloped in his scent. In that instant, she had no idea why she hadn't done this before. The sensation of his fingers on her arm earlier was nothing compared to the touch of his lips on hers.

Marc took all of a nanosecond to wrap his arms around her waist and pull her tight to his body. Disorientation swept through her. As revenge sex went, this was not going to suck.

"We can't go to my place. How's yours?" she murmured, unwilling to lean back far enough to take in his expression.

"Let's go." He stood, carrying her with him. When he set her on her feet, he pulled her tight against his side. Her shoulder fit under his arm like they were designed as a matching pair. She couldn't help but put her arm around his back. "I parked at the diner."

"Great." That path led them right past where Roger was skulking right at the edge of the light cast by a street lamp. *That's right, you bastard. Just watch and remember because you can't have your cake and eat it, too. This cake just got picked off the bakery shelf by someone who wanted to take her home for real.*

None of that made any sense either, but Roger's expression of mingled horror, desperation, and lust canceled out her own disgust with her wordsmithing. He followed them to Marc's car where Marc pressed her against the passenger door before he opened it. Heat at the soft touch of his lips swelled through her. Roger was watching. The best revenge.

Then they were headed up the mountain, and she realized she was going to have to have sex with him. She could say no, but that wasn't her normal brand of stupid. She'd been specializing in saying yes, and this yes could be the best one ever. Alex studied Marc. He was focused on the road, giving her a window to observe. The only man she'd ever made love to was Roger. Marc was younger, fitter. It would be interesting to compare them. And women did this. It wasn't humiliating or shameful to go home with a man on the second date. Even if it was, she'd already done worse, and it wasn't like anyone was going to pin two scarlet letter As on her chest.

In front of a huge house, halfway up the mountain, Marc parked the car. Fumbling with keys, he opened the front door of the house and turned to her the second she stepped through.

He pressed her against the wall, lifting her to her toes as he nuzzled her neck. Everything about him was hard. Alex drew her fingers down his back. He didn't remind her not to leave evidence on him. Oh, yeah. "Marc?"

"Where do you want to go, baby? Here, there?" He lifted his face enough to let her see the couch in the sunken living room.

Wow, this house was amazing. "Everywhere?"

He laughed and scooped her off her feet.

Alex grabbed for his shoulders as a wave of dizziness rattled her. Rock hard shoulders. There wasn't a soft spot on the man. He carried her to the couch and laid her down.

"I'm glad you decided to extend the evening." Marc stroked her cheek with the back of his finger.

"I wasn't doing anything with it."

He kissed her, stealing her breath.

Alex didn't think she'd ever want to do anything else ever again. His fingers searched under the hem of her shirt, calluses dragging across her skin like molten heat. She arched to draw him farther in. He groaned. The vibration settled in her belly. She hooked her fingers inside the waistband of his jeans, trying to work her way to the button, but his body pressed too tight to hers. Getting closer was going to require separating. "We're overdressed."

"What?" His voice had a very rewarding groggy quality.

"The clothes. There are too many of them."

He growled and leaned back to pull off his shirt. When he started to lean in again, Alex slithered away.

"Where are you going?"

She smirked. Positioning herself in front of him, she toyed with the hem of her white T-shirt. That clued him in. Marc sat up on the couch, kicked off his sneakers, and stretched his long legs out on either side of her. Undulating, Alex drew the shirt over her head. For an instant, she was blinded by the material. The sound of the wind soughing through the trees competed with Marc's husky breaths. Then she shook her head free of the shirt and caught sight of his face. The fact that it wasn't Roger, and this wasn't his crowded office in the English building, surprised her for a split second. Marc reached for her so she danced backward a step.

"Still too many clothes."

"We can take care of that together." He leaned forward and caught one of her belt loops. Before he could reel her in, she opened the button, so he could slide her jeans and underwear down her legs before pulling her under him.

"My feet are stuck in my shoes." That didn't hinder anything. Why the hell had she brought it up?

Marc sat up and shook his head. "Are you always going to be this difficult?"

"Difficult? I only made you buy me two ice cream cones before I'd have sex with you."

"Fair enough." He slid off the couch and untangled her feet from her shoes and jeans. "To be honest, I prefer to have a woman's legs wrapped around my hips when she's screaming."

"I'll work on that."

Marc shucked his own jeans, affording her a moment to drink in the sight of him as he slid on a condom he had produced like a magic trick. Everything about him looked as hard as it felt. Velvet over steel. Fine, high quality velvet over the kind of steel used to build skyscrapers. Then everything was obliterated by the sensation of him on her and in her and all around her. Alex caught the wave and held on. Her fingers sunk into his skin as the tension rode up and down her body until it tightened, then broke in a rush.

"Good. Good," Marc murmured. "Nice touch with the legs."

Alex pried her eyes open. When had she wrapped her arms around his shoulders and her legs around his hips? Better question, how the hell was she going to get loose? Her ankles had knotted together in some kind of complicated maritime knot that would require a dozen Eagle Scouts to undo. Not that she was letting any scouts see her in this condition. "Thanks. I thought you'd appreciate it." She flexed an ankle. Maybe they would unravel on their own.

"Am I crushing you?" He started to slip sideways.

"No, not at all." It felt good. Alarmingly good. Crushed into this very soft couch by this very strong man.

Dear God, what was she doing here? Her ankles unwrapped themselves like someone had spoken the magic words.

Marc rose up on his elbows, sliding down her body a few precious inches and lifting the bulk of his weight off her, which both relieved and disappointed her. "So listen, it's just you and me here if you want to stay the night and we can work on that here, there, and everywhere thing. Or I can drive you back to town if you want."

"Town?" The last place she wanted to be was down in the valley. She wanted to be here. Right here. For the rest of her life. Hiding and letting herself be used by this man however he wanted. Commitments always got in the way. Job, classes, wives. "I have breakfast in the morning."

Marc cupped her breast, stroking her nipple through the bra they'd never bothered to remove. "I'm pretty sure there's some form of breakfast food in the house."

"No, at the diner. I open."

He flinched. "What time?"

"Six."

Marc winced for sure this time. "I could drive you down in the morning."

"Yeah. I bet you're all excited about seeing the sun rise over the mountains." Alex wiggled away from him.

"I can do it."

"You don't have to." Alex pulled on her jeans. She needed to learn to set boundaries. With him and with herself. She also needed a little time to process this development. Besides six a.m. was close. "If you could give me a ride to my cousin's house, I'd appreciate it. It's a long walk."

"Of course I will." He stood up and wrapped his arms around her. Still naked. Still nice to touch. "What time are you finished?"

"Two."

"I'll come for a late lunch and get you then." He grazed his warm lips across her temple. "We can get to work on that here, there, and everywhere thing tomorrow."

Heat spilled along her limbs, wanting to drag her to the couch under him. "Okay. I have the day after off."

"Great."

Chapter 5

"I thought it was good the way it was." Marc paced across the living room. Jason had a gift for interfering with his pursuit of Alex.

"I think it could be better."

He checked his watch. "It's fucking brilliant now. Look, I'm kinda busy at the moment. Give me a couple of days with it." Shithead. Woke up in the middle of the night with a brilliant riff and demanded three hours on the phone hammering out a brilliant song, but Jason wanted more. He wanted to be the hardest working man in show business. But why was it so horribly timed?

"A couple of days? What's her name?"

"Alex." Alex, the deer he was trying to get to eat out of his hand. He'd gotten that far. Now he needed to domesticate her so she would eat out of his hand all the time.

Jason snickered. "Oh, that's right. I forgot about her. Have fun. Don't forget to change the sheets. Cassie wanted me to remind you about it." Jason hung up.

Jason had been a lot easier to deal with since Cassie came into his life. She was nice enough, except for her weird obsession with sheets.

His phone rang in his hand and he answered. "Yeah?"

"Hey, it's me."

"Yes, Jason, it's you. We just talked."

"I know, but I forgot to tell you my big news."

Marc's gut tightened. What else was going swimmingly in Jason's perfect life? "What's that?"

"Cassie's pregnant. I'm gonna have another kid in about eight months."

"That's great." Marc hoped the sound of his teeth grinding couldn't be heard through the phone. The connection could not be that clear. "Tell her I said congratulations."

"I will. I'm pretty excited."

"Yeah, that's great. I'm happy for you. I'll talk to you later, okay?"

"Sure. Have fun."

Marc dropped his phone on the table and walked out to his car. Better to leave the phone here so he could focus on Alex. If Jason followed form—and there was no reason to believe he wouldn't—he'd forgotten to tell anyone else about Cassie's pregnancy in his obsession with his new ditty. He was likely, right now, on the phone with Brian spreading the good cheer, followed by a call to Bear, and then Ty, who might find time between recovering from last night and getting ready to go out tonight, to make a call. Marc took solace in that Brian would be as excited about the pregnancy as he was. Already saddled with two monsters of his own and divorced, Brian wouldn't want to see his best pal headed down the same path. Though it wasn't the same path. Not really. Cassie was nothing like Bonnie. She was a great mom to their little girl, and she was long haul material unlike Dez, who had never earned Tessa's lawyerly seal of approval. Who knew what Bear would say. Cruising into his third year with Maureen, they seemed happy enough, but in no rush to have kids. Ty would say congratulations and run out to have a vasectomy. Then there was the management company. And the assorted hangers-on. Ugh, SendDown was in the studio so there would be separate calls from each of them as the "happy" news spread. On tour, Savitar would all learn at once so that would only entail one call, plus Suzi, from that camp.

Fantastic. He was going to come home with Alex to a whole passel of excited messages, texts, and e-mails, and their next album was going to be delayed for at least a year. His entire life was stalled.

Once upon a time, he and Dez had talked about having children. Then she started cheating on him with her personal trainer the tour before last. At one point, he'd wanted kids, but between Dez and Brian's less than bucolic experience, maybe he needed to rethink that notion.

Jason's song was headed in a very upbeat direction. Nothing he could work with in this mood.

Ida smirked at him when he pushed through the diner door. "Well, surprise, surprise." She sounded like Gomer Pyle on *The Andy Griffith Show.* "Eating inside today? As if I didn't know."

"Yeah. How are you doing? Aren't you supposed to be home resting?"

"It was just a panic attack. Believe me, I'm going to be a lot more panicked sitting at home worrying about what's going on here."

Marc folded his arms. "Ida, you have to take care of yourself before your business. You go down and so does it."

"That's not what yesterday's receipts say. Thanks for stepping in. Alex said you were a big help."

"Nothing you wouldn't have done in my place."

Ida laughed. "Can you see me going on stage and playing a guitar in front of those fans of yours? I'd get booed off the stage."

"You know how to entertain a crowd." He grinned at her. When Jason announced he was building a house here, everyone thought he'd lost his mind, but it had a special appeal. "It was nothing."

"Plus you got to work with Alex."

"There was that."

"Thought so. Any special requests you want me to relay to the kitchen?"

"No."

She snickered in a very self-satisfied way, handed him his personal coffee mug, and pointed to a booth along the wall that was empty despite every other seat in the place being filled. Marc still wondered where Ida had managed to lay hands on a Paul McCartney and Wings coffee mug for him.

Alex was waiting on a couple in the back who were cooing at each other so much Marc wasn't sure how she got an order out of them. Eventually, she freed herself to come to his table with a carafe of coffee. "If you want decaf, I'll have to go get it."

"Whatever you have is fine."

Alex's lips curled into a suggestive smile. "Is that so?"

He couldn't stop himself from answering that smile promise for promise. "It is."

"So, am I putting an order in for you or does Paul already know what you want?" she asked, pouring the coffee.

"I'll take the chef's choice."

"Very good, sir. I'll go let him know." As she turned away from the table, she gave her hips a little twist that made his groin tighten.

Ida slid into the booth across from him. "So, we were right."

"About?"

"You and Alex. She's a fine girl."

"Yeah, she is."

"She's off tomorrow. You'll have her all to your wicked self all day."

Ida was a nice lady, but talking about this with her was like talking to his grandma about sex. He needed her off the topic and no sacrifice was too great.

"Did you hear the news?"

"What news?"

"Cassie's pregnant again. Jason said she's due in eight months."

Ida clapped her hands once, somehow managing to not carve herself up with her long, green talons. "Really? I have to call her mama. She said they were going to try again, but I didn't think it would take so soon." Ida scuttled away.

That Jason and Cassie had decided to try for another kid was news to Marc. How many kids did they want? Jason had four sisters and two half sisters, but his family was sort of a train wreck. Cassie's family was composed of her and her parents.

Alex came out of the kitchen with a tray in her hands. She delivered it to a table with a family of four. He watched her sorting out their orders like a pro and getting the kids set up with straws in their drinks and crayons brushed to the side where they wouldn't wind up in the ketchup. What kind of family did she come from? What kind of family did she want?

What kind of lunatic was he thinking about this based on a one night stand?

Still, she handled the kids like she knew what she was doing and was comfortable with it. They both had dark hair and brown eyes, tall, thin. Their kids had a very high probability of being good looking and intelligent. He could have something to look forward to when he came home from tour other than a cold house and a note from the housekeeper that she'd stocked him with milk and bread, but he'd have to call if he wanted anything else. If he was going to be thinking this way at all, he needed to get Tessa on the usual background checks or she'd have his head on a platter.

"What?" Alex had appeared at the side of his table and was looking at him funny.

Marc blinked. "Nothing."

"You had an odd look on your face."

"Just thinking." That song of Jason's wasn't so difficult to put lyrics to. It started bubbling around in his head as he looked at her. That bright focused smile that hadn't been practiced in a mirror to impress him after the show. It was genuine. Marc grabbed her wrist and dragged her into the booth next to him.

"What are you doing?" She pulled away. "You're going to give the yokels ideas."

"I'll have them killed if they touch you." Something black reared up in his chest. If anyone touched her wrong, he might have to kill them himself.

"Yeah, I'm honored, but hiring hit men is a little extreme." Alex stood up. "I just came over to tell you that Paul is making you eggs Benedict. He says you look thin. I'll bring it right out and then I'm turning my tables over to Drew for the rest of the day."

"You having lunch with me? Because you're going to need your strength." He grinned.

Alex laughed. She had a great, musical laugh. "Here, there, and everywhere." Then she headed for the kitchen.

* * * *

"Did you tell his majesty what I told you to tell him?" Paul demanded as soon as she walked through the door.

"Yes." Most of it. She hadn't mentioned that in addition to Marc looking thin, he needed a good woman to take care of him. Too bad she wasn't that good woman. Nobody was going to be calling her a good woman anytime soon. Alex fished her tips out of her apron pockets before tossing it in the hamper inside the back door.

"What did he say?"

"He asked if I was going to eat with him."

Paul's lips curled into a Cheshire smile. "Excellent."

"Hey, Alex," Tina said, walking in the out door from the outside seating area. Twice already this summer, she'd done that, and Drew had ended up with a face full of food both times. "There's a guy out here who asked to talk to you."

"Tina, you have to mind the doors," Paul snapped.

"Oh, sorry." Tina frowned at the doors like they were at fault.

"Is it a customer?" Alex asked.

"Is what a customer?"

"The guy who wants to talk to me."

"I've never seen him before."

That didn't narrow the field much. If he wasn't a townie, Tina didn't know him. Otherwise he could have been anyone from the President of the United States to the postmaster two towns over. That field included Roger. Crap. "What does he look like?"

"Chubby, dark hair. He's right over there by the bench at the sidewalk." Tina pointed out the door.

Alex's hands went cold. Roger. That nice warm feeling that had been pooling in her belly at the thought of going home with Marc froze solid. She threw open the out door hard enough that it banged on the wall and raced across the concrete as fast as walking would allow.

Roger had been seated on the far edge of Tina's section, almost on the sidewalk. He smiled and reached for her when she skidded to a stop in front of him.

Alex put her hands behind her back and laced her fingers together for good measure. "What are you doing here?"

"I missed you, my darling."

"Did you now?"

"Alex, don't be like this."

Alex raised an eyebrow.

Roger nodded. "I understand. You're angry. I can make it up to you."

"You can make it up to me by going back to your wife."

"You know I don't love her. I just can't leave her now. Not with the new baby."

Alex clenched her fingers together. "I don't want you to leave your wife for me."

"But I don't love her. I love you."

Alex forced herself to take even breaths. This is why she had needed to get off campus for the summer. His arguments made sense when he made them in person. She needed the distance to let logic work. She took a step backward. "So you keep telling me, but whether you love me or not is immaterial. I'm not going to be responsible for destroying your family anymore than I already have."

"Carla has destroyed my family. I am doing my best for my children."

"You don't need me to do the best for your children."

"But I do. I love you. You give me the strength to go on. I can't live without you."

Her battle plan of even breathing faltered. "You wouldn't do anything irrevocable, would you?" Him dying for her had to be worse than him leaving his wife for her. That's what she'd been telling herself for the last three years, every time she had told him they were done, and he'd made his veiled threats.

"I can't survive without you. My life is a barren wasteland." He held out a manila envelope. "This is for you."

"What is it?"

"Your master's thesis. I can turn it in now and make sure it gets approved before fall semester starts. There's still time to get a freshman English class."

Alex stared at the envelope. Her thesis. She'd planned on spending most, if not all, of next semester working on it so she could get a teaching post, maybe next year. Then she'd have her toe in the door for a real faculty position. Working side by side with Roger. Somehow that didn't have the same draw it used to. "You finished my thesis?"

"No, this was an unfinished one that I found."

Someone misplaced a master's thesis and didn't check the lost and found? That wouldn't happen. No one would get most of the way through a master's thesis and just abandon it. No one had dropped out of the program in the last three years or she'd have heard. "Who's is it?"

"Melanie Finch."

"Melanie—Melanie Finch? What did you do? Raid her room and steal her notes after she committed suicide last Christmas?"

"No, she was working on it before then. I just finished it up for you."

"She was writing about Sylvia Plath."

Roger shrugged. "We'll tell the committee that you changed your topic after Melanie died because she was such a good friend."

"I barely knew Melanie." That warm pool in her stomach that had frozen when Tina had told her Roger was here was now splintering and stabbing at her gut. He stole a paper from a dead girl in an effort to woo back his mistress after she finally managed to get enough backbone together to really call it off this time. Alex didn't recall auditioning for a soap opera, but here she was. "Roger, you need to go."

"I saw you last night with that young man."

Young man? Oh. "That's my boyfriend." Or at the very least the guy she liked and who she was pretty sure liked her back in a very honest and above board way.

"I see." Roger's mouth tightened. "I'm surprised to see a man like that with you."

Alex licked her lips, allowing herself a moment to let his phasing sink in. A man like Marc. Clever, kind, willing to be seen in public with her. No, she didn't deserve a man like Marc, but she didn't deserve a man like Roger either, no matter what she'd done in the past. "He's the same age as you are."

Roger winced. In comparison, Marc looked two hundred times hotter. "Alex, please, I can make this right. You know he's going to leave you. I would never abandon you. I love you."

Alex's fingers ached from being clenched together so long. His shoulders sagged, so bereft that she wanted to put her arms around him and tell him everything would be all right. Old habits died hard. She needed to ask Marc about hiring hit men for them. "You need to go. Your wife is probably wondering where you are."

"She's visiting her family in Connecticut. I told her I was coming here to get some peace and quiet to work on my book."

"You're staying in town?"

"I got a cabin at the In the Pines campground on the mountain."

"You should go home." Alex turned and started back toward the restaurant.

"'The sedge has withered from the lake. And no birds sing.'"

Alex forced her feet to keep moving forward. "Quoting Keats to me won't help this time, Roger." Not if he was going to quote *La Belle Dame Sans Merci*. Calling a woman merciless wasn't the best way to win her back, even if she wanted to return.

Paul had their food plated and waiting when she walked back in. "Who was that?"

"My master's advisor. I can't believe you put the food on the plates before I got in here. What happened to the freshest possible presentation?" Alex shifted the hot plates to a tray with a bright pink silicone potholder.

"I plated them when I saw you start back this way. Hurry up or those eggs are going to overcook just sitting there."

He was watching her. Of course he was watching her. A teeny, tiny gossipy town and her biggest scandal was wandering around with a stolen master's thesis.

"You know Marc is a better man," Paul said when she was halfway through the door where she couldn't respond.

The worst part was—she did know. The way Marc's gaze followed her as she worked her way across the dining room with their lunch like there wasn't another woman on the planet for him. She wasn't *his* dirty little secret. The frozen pool in her belly thawed and started to simmer. "Hungry?"

"For whatever you have."

She slid the plate in front of him. "So what's the plan for this afternoon?"

"I thought we could go back to the house and get to know each other better."

"Or we could just have sex."

"Or we could do that." He grinned and dug into his eggs.

* * * *

Alex brushed her fingers around Marc's shoulder. Sun poured through the open window, bringing with it the sound of the waterfall on the other side of the house. A breeze lifted the buttercup yellow curtains while birds chirped outside. Honeysuckle growing up the side of the house scented the room. Crisp white sheets on a dark mahogany sleigh bed. Marc's chest rose and fell under her cheek as his breath slowed to a normal rhythm. His arm draped down her back so that his hand rested on her bare hip. He brushed his lips across her temple. "Good?"

If he only knew. She was happy to have sex in a bed. "Very good."

He chuckled. "Good."

"Marc?"

"Yeah, babe?"

"Why me?"

"What do you mean, why you?" His hand slid up and around her waist, tugging her closer.

"Why did you pick me out of all the available women in town?" In the world.

"You came highly recommended." He brushed his lips across her temple.

"By Paul and Ida."

"Sure, and Angela."

"But you could have ignored them."

"They were very convincing."

"Oh." And that was enough for him. Like getting suggestions when buying a new car. Should she ask if she was just a weekend rental or a long-term lease? No, that was too much like a relationship conversation. Roger always hated those talks. According to all the women's magazines, men in general hated them. Which left her with nothing to talk about. The beautiful, scented, and soft room morphed into a dungeon of silence. What if he was waiting for her to say something? What if he was starting to think she was some kind of idiot because she wasn't talking? Crap. "So how did you end up connected to Potterville?"

"What?"

He sounded half asleep. Shit, she should have kept quiet. "I just wondered how you ended up here. It's not a big deal."

"A buddy of mine married a woman from here and built this house for her. He had a guest cabin built just below this and a studio building behind the house so the band could come out here to record. Cassie still owns the campground next door, too."

"There's a campground next door?" Alex couldn't see out the window from here. There was a good-sized cabin down the mountain a little way with a set of stairs leading up here. Now that she thought about it, she remembered seeing an oversized shed through the kitchen windows. Other than that, it was trees on all sides.

"There's a path through the trees that connects them, but you have to know where it is otherwise there would be fans here all the time. There's also a locked gate and a fence. You'd have to have climbing equipment to get to the house from there without the key. Don't worry about the fans."

And why would she when he was making such a big deal about how they weren't a danger? Unless he'd had stalkers in the past. The ones she'd seen in town hadn't seemed so bad. The only really dangerous person in town was Roger, and the worst he could do was out her.

Or kill himself, which was turning out to be an emptier threat all the time. Instead, he'd chased her here with a stolen thesis. She needed to get off this train of thought before it crashed into something.

"How did he meet her?"

"We exiled him." Marc shifted, curving his body to hers. "He had just broken up with this coat hanger he'd been living with and was being a pain in the ass."

Since his friend was probably not in a serious relationship with a wire coat hanger, he must mean a very thin woman. Did that suggest that he didn't like skinny women? It wasn't like she hadn't tried to gain a little weight; it just never stuck to the right places.

"So we shipped him off to the In the Pines Campground to cool his heels before we murdered him and stuffed him under the drum riser."

Every muscle in Alex's body wound tight. "What was the name of the campground?"

"In the Pines. That's the title of Cassie's dad's favorite song, so she named her campground after it."

Crash.

In the Pines Campground. Where Roger was "working on his book." And it was right next door. Alex sat up so fast her head spun. "I'm going to go take a shower."

Marc trailed his fingers down her spine. "Towels are in the cupboard."

She forced herself to walk across the room like a normal person. No hunching, no scurrying, no whimpering. Inside the white and yellow bathroom, she tried to shut the door sanely, but it slipped at the last second and slammed. "Sorry. Wind caught it."

"I'm gonna go downstairs." The floor creaked.

"Okay." From where she was leaning against the door like Marc was a vicious killer about to come after her, she could see her reflection in the mirror. Was that flush from recent sex or from panicked flight? Dear God, she did look like a coat hanger. But he had to know she wasn't starving herself. She had eaten as much as he had at lunch.

Roger was at the campground next door with a stolen master's thesis. He might find his way over here and tell Marc about them. Alex fanned her face. Paranoia was goosing her imagination. Marc said there was a fence, and the trail between the campground and the fence was hidden. Roger would also have had to know who Marc was, and Roger knew less about popular music than she did. Roger was a jazz guy.

Alex stepped under the stream. She needed a good rinse to wash the crazy out.

By the time she got to the living room, he was on the phone and watching a baseball game on the big screen TV in the corner. No Roger lurking at the windows. The house only lacked for decent reading material. There was a shelf in the living room with a few bestsellers on it, but nothing interesting. She could pull out the Percy Bysshe Shelley bio she was reading. Marc might even want to talk about it. Shelley and Byron were rock stars in their day. Marc might have some good insights on the joys of being mobbed by adoring fans.

No, her brain hurt from a long breakfast shift and all those conspiracy theories she was building in the bathroom. She didn't have the mental fortitude to digest Shelley or discuss his history.

Marc didn't seem to care what she did. He was involved in his game and his phone call. He didn't need to have someone hanging on his every breath. Being with him was easy. He wasn't making demands other than the ones she enjoyed fulfilling. She could learn to like this for however long it lasted.

Chapter 6

Marc switched off the TV. Alex had fallen asleep against him. She was going to wake up with crazy hair. That was kinda cool. He couldn't remember the last woman he met who wasn't obsessed with her appearance. Even Maureen, who was about the most mellow woman he'd ever met, had issues with what she would or wouldn't wear in public. He leaned his head on Alex's. Paul had said she was pretty together. It was nice to hang with a woman who wasn't getting all neurotic on him.

His phone rang with Dez's ringtone, and like an idiot, he answered. The point of giving her the Darth Vader theme was so he wouldn't pick up when she called. "What do you want now, Dez?"

"Who says I want anything, baby?"

"Pattern of behavior. What do you want?"

"I was just missing you is all. We had some good times."

"Until you started fucking around with your personal trainer on my dime." Alex shifted so Marc forced himself to relax. No need to wake her up by getting angry at the ex.

"I told you, baby. I was lonely."

He had to stop answering her calls. Damn Jody for giving her the number. Now he was going to have to get a new one. "How much do you need?"

"I need you, baby."

She needed his checkbook. The allowance he'd given her had paid for her lifestyle. "Dez, cut the bullshit."

"You know, I never got mad at you when you cheated on me."

"That's because I never cheated on you."

"Oh, come on now." Dez's voice dropped into the sexy, wheedling purr that used to drive him crazy in all the right ways. Yeah, not working so much now. "There had to be one or two on those long, long tours."

"Nope, not one. I promised to be faithful to you, and I was." Lots of cold showers. A couple of porn-per-view movies. Many, many conversations with Bear about quality. All of which had netted him a cheating wife while Bear waited around to bump into the love of his life and had fun doing it. "Dez, the bank is closed and so is the bedroom door. I told you how I felt about cheating when we got married. You broke the deal. Now I want you to stop calling me or I'm going to have to take legal action."

Nothing.

"Dez?"

Still nothing.

Marc glared at the phone. "Bitch."

"Who was that?"

"My ex-wife."

"What did she do?" Alex asked.

"She hung up on me." He chucked the phone on the table. It slid all the way across and fell off the other side. He should have done that when it rang instead of answering.

Alex sat up and ran her fingers through her hair. "To become the ex, she had an affair?"

"You make it sound almost classy. She hooked up with her personal trainer while I was on tour and the dude cannot abide." How much did it suck the bitch could wind him up this bad after so long. Maybe his office manager Helen was right, and he did love her. Either that or his drummer Bear was right, and he hated to lose.

He really hated to lose.

"What?"

Marc turned to Alex. Oh, right, he had a woman here with him. He shouldn't be dwelling on the ex. "I just can't stand cheaters. I've seen a lot of people ripped apart by cheaters."

"So you're a monogamy advocate." She leaned back against the arm of the couch and crossed her arms. Her hair was screwed up from falling asleep with it wet, and she didn't seem to care. She was also not lowballing him with questions packed with single syllable words about where his ideas came from. Cool.

"Not really. I think once you say "I do," it's part of the deal, but if everybody knows the score, it's your private life."

"You value honesty then."

"You could say that. My buddy Ty used to date Candy, she's our publicist, but he wanted to play the field and she wanted him to be hers and hers alone. He couldn't do it, so they broke up. We all still work together, and it's okay because they were honest about it."

Alex frowned. "You make it sound like they had a rational conversation over coffee."

"No, if I remember correctly there was a huge screaming argument in a hotel hallway in the middle of the night during of one of those endless tours we did at the beginning." Marc shrugged. "But Ty has always been kind of an idiot. Lucky for him, singers are hard to replace."

"But they were honest about it."

"Sure. After a while."

"Are they back together?"

"No. There's no hope for them as a couple. What she wants and what he wants are diametrically opposed." God, he sounded like an old man. Hot girl half naked on the couch next to him and he was waxing poetic about thousand-year-old gossip. He grinned. "'And these are the days of our lives.'"

"So what are you looking for?"

"Now?"

She nodded.

The love of my life. Somebody willing to be as true to me as Maureen was to Bear. That would go over beautifully with the bright young thing on the other end of the couch taking pity on his old ass. "Fun with an option for long term. You?"

She shrugged. "That's acceptable." Then she jumped up. "I'm starving. Is there anything to eat around here?"

Something else she wasn't obsessed with. He wouldn't have to listen to Alex complain about being full after a side salad and wake up in the middle of the night to find her stuffing her face from a convenience store bag. "Depends on how hungry you are. I don't eat in much." He followed her to the kitchen.

"I noticed." Alex was standing in front of a cupboard studying the contents, an open box of Ritz crackers.

"I can call the diner and have something brought up if you don't want to go into town. Or I could call the grocery store and have them bring up something from the deli."

Alex shrugged, still staring into the cupboard. "'No legacy is so rich as honesty.'"

Marc leaned to one side so he could get a better angle into the cupboard. Everything had been going so nicely. That was the end of that. "What?"

"What?" Alex turned around, closing the cupboard as she did, and smiled at him. "It's Shakespeare. It popped into my head."

"Okay."

"I have a confession to make."

Shit, here it came. All that big talk about honesty when he should have just kept his mouth shut and enjoyed the ride. There were four honest women on the planet, and two were married to other guys in his band, one was Suzi who was in a serious relationship with that dipwad from Savitar, and the last was Tessa who was about as likely to settle down as a plastic bag in a windstorm.

"I knew who you were before we hooked up." Alex flexed her fingers like she was warming up to play a grand piano. "Not when I first met you, but before you came into the diner after we closed that night and you fixed the dishwasher. I mean, you couldn't walk down the street for about three years without hearing that 'Lucky Charmer' song."

"And?"

She shrugged. The material of her T-shirt tugged around her small breasts. "That's it. I just played it like I had no clue who you were, and I did it because I figured you want a woman who wasn't after you for what you are."

Marc thought the breeze from the train that had nearly hit him should be ruffling his hair at least, but there was nothing. When Bear and Maureen met, he remembered telling Bear he'd never find a woman who loved him for who *he* was instead of who he *was*. In his head, it had made sense, but Maureen did love Bear for himself and not his bank balance or his connections. The unicorn did exist. So Alex knew who he was around the time she met him. That was more believable than her not knowing who he was at all. She didn't appear to be after anything more substantial than stale crackers. "No harm done. Now, what were we talking about?"

She smiled. "We were talking about food."

"I thought we were."

She sauntered across the kitchen and put her arms around his neck. "We could talk about something else."

"Like?" Her body pressed against his, warm and delicious, but he couldn't shake the feeling that he'd missed something in the conversation. Like the point.

She rose up on her toes. "Shakespeare."

That was one hell of a sexy name and the point was overrated. Half of Potterville hadn't been trying to fix him up with a life partner. They'd been arranging a nice summer vacation for him, and everybody knew it up front. He wrapped his arms around her waist. "I thought you were hungry."

"Peckish, but I could be distracted."

So could he. Marc tasted her lips. He scooped her up and carried her back to the couch. She stretched her arms over her head thrusting her small, round breasts up, already tensed for his touch. Marc lay down next to her. "Alex?"

Her eyes were dark and focused on his like she'd devour him if she could. "Shh." She pulled him down to kiss her as she guided his hand under her shirt.

His fingers glossed over her soft skin as the heat of her mouth plied him. Something had been bugging him a minute ago, but damned if he could remember. Her leg coiled over his, pulling him on top of her. It was like drowning and loving it. She broke their kiss to shift to his ear. Her hot breath made him shiver. He'd never been with a woman like this. Alex had a single-minded passion he'd never encountered. She was a level beyond any groupie he'd ever been with. Her hands reached into the waistband of his jeans at the back, working their way around to the zipper. He needed to move before he lost control of this encounter.

Before she could get him undone, he slid down her body, pushing her shirt up at the same time. No bra to get in the way. Her creamy pale skin accented her pink nipples. "Have I mentioned how smokin' hot you are?"

"Once or twice."

He laved his tongue across her nipple. She dug her fingernails into his shoulders. She made little gasping noises like she was smothering herself. He'd get a scream out of her yet. He pushed her shorts and panties down, dragging them the rest of the way off as he licked his way down her smooth flat belly.

"No, no we can't." She twisted as if she wanted to escape, but he caught her hips and kissed the inside of her thigh. She wilted on the cushions, still making those desperate little gasps. He spread her open with his thumbs, searching for her rose bud. The first taste was sweeter than he'd imagined, and as he worked her with his lips and tongue, her gasps deepened to strangled moans before she tensed and arched. The only way he knew she'd climaxed was when she slumped, panting.

Marc eased his way up beside her.

She blinked at him and smiled, her skin sweaty. "Your turn?"

"We'll let this one be about you."

Alex opened her mouth and then closed it again. With a deep sigh, she snuggled her cheek into his chest and closed her eyes.

She never made noise when they had sex. He couldn't tell her it bothered him enough that he'd lost steam altogether. There was honesty, and then there was unnecessary roughness.

Some women didn't make a lot of noise during sex, but Alex always sounded like she was forcing herself to stay quiet. Most of the ones he'd known went out of their way to be as noisy as possible. Could be linked to the deep dark secret relationship everyone said she'd just gotten out of. What the hell could she have done? Hooked up with a girl? If that was her thing, whatever, but she might be embarrassed about it. Damn, what if he was her beard? That would suck, but what the hell else could it be? Something was rotten in the state of Denmark.

* * * *

Alex propped her chin on her fist. Marc rolled the dice. She'd barely bested him at Scrabble. When he had started with *ant* as his first word, she'd figured it was going to be a slaughter until he had turned it into *vagrant* on the next turn and sneaked ahead. From there, it had been neck and neck until she started throwing tiles into his lap to distract him, and he refused to play the game anymore so they had switched to Monopoly. Birds chirped outside the window as he worked out whatever complex calculations he needed to decide what to do next.

"Damn." He shifted his tiny Scottie dog to Park Place. "I think I'm out. What's the rent?"

"More than you have in the whole wide game." Alex grinned at him.

"I don't understand how you did it. I was killing you at first."

"That was when you started taking sexual favors as rent."

"You had no money."

Alex slid her hand under the board and pulled out her stash. By this point, the colorful pile was pretty bulky.

"When did you do that?"

"I took half my money at the beginning of the game and tucked it under there for emergencies."

"And you had me giving you advice on how to play." Marc glared at her playfully. "You lied to me."

"No, I didn't know how to play. I just like to have a cushion. But it was very sweet of you to remind me to buy every property I landed on."

"Including the one you just beat me with." He reached across the board and slid his hand around the back of her neck. "Cheater."

"This is caution, not cheating." She allowed him to draw her closer, focused on covering the fluster he brought on by calling her a cheater.

He brushed his lips across hers. "Let's get this cleaned up before we end up with play money all over the room."

"Well, we don't want to have to replace all of Jason's games."

"It wasn't my idea to start throwing Scrabble tiles." Marc swept up the money and sorted it with his long fingers before sliding it into the plastic tray. "So you want to go to Italy."

"Is that a question or a statement?" Alex put away the pieces and folded the board. Just when she was acclimating to temporary joy, he had to bring up future plans. It had taken half the Scrabble game before she'd been able to stop ruminating on that long-term option thing, and now she had the cheater thing chewing on her subconscious.

"You said you wanted to go to Italy. I was thinking."

"A first for everything." Maybe that would break his focus and get him off the subject.

He slid the lid on the box and picked it up. "My buddy's wife is expecting so I'm not going to be doing much work for at least the next year. Can you take time off from your school stuff?"

"I'd have to pay tuition for the semester." The math superseded the subconscious cheater rumination. The whole point of coming here this summer had been to earn money to pay for school, and if she didn't go back in the fall, all her student loans were going to crash down on her head.

He shrugged.

Of course, a measly semester of tuition would be pocket change to him, and what was a hundred grand in school loans when she could spend more time with Marc? It wasn't as if he loved her. "I suppose I could."

"Let me take you to Italy for a couple of months."

Alex blinked. He could not have said what she thought he said. "Months?"

"Why? Don't you want to take that much time off?" He slid the game box back on its shelf and turned to her, all tall and lean with a serious look on his face.

"Italy. For months."

"Do you think we'll need four months? I was thinking three, but it's a whole country and there is a lot to see." No hint of a smirk to tell her he was joking.

"No, I mean you want to spend months in just Italy."

"You said you wanted to go there. Is there someplace else you want to go?"

Alex licked her lips. Still no hint that he might be joking. "What about my job at the university? If I quit, I won't be able to pay for tuition spring semester either. And all my loans will come due."

"That's true." Marc shoved his hands in his pockets and cocked his head. "I guess I'm getting a little ahead of things. What do you want to do now?"

"Throw myself off a cliff because I think I just screwed myself out of a trip to Italy by being practical." Oh jeez, she'd said that out loud.

Marc laughed. "Unlikely."

What the hell did that mean? Roger, for all his disaster and misery, was at least predictable. Hurried sex on the desk. Invisible to him in public. He couldn't live without her, but he couldn't leave Carla. Around and around like a really terrible carnival ride.

Marc was much better, but unpredictable.

"Is there any of that chicken left?" Marc headed for the kitchen.

"They brought up an entire chicken dinner for six. Of course there's chicken left." She crawled over to a shelf of DVDs.

"I'm making a sandwich," he called from the kitchen. "You want?"

"Sure."

"Mustard or mayo?"

"Mayo." It was a much broader collection than the books. No *Mary Shelley's Frankenstein,* though.

"There's no mayo."

"Then why did you ask?"

"To tease you."

"There are better ways for you to do that."

"Eat first, then I'll practice various ways of teasing you."

"Promises, promises."

He leaned around the arch from the kitchen. "Oh, darlin', it's a guarantee. That's a good one. You want to watch it?"

Alex read at the box in her hand. *Airplane!* It looked stupid to her, but if he liked it, fine. It would fill time so she didn't have to worry about what to talk about. "Sure. I'm peach-eating this week."

"Nuked or not nuked?"

"Surprise me."

The microwave door popped open and closed, then he stepped out of the kitchen. "You're what this week?"

"Peach-eating."

He shook his head. "Never heard that one before. Educate me."

He'd said the same in the middle of Scrabble when she'd turned *robe* into *chifforobe* and he had wanted to know the meaning. Good thing there was an excellent film version of *To Kill a Mockingbird*.

"It's from a poem, 'The Love Song of J. Alfred Prufrock.' That's what I'm doing my master's on."

"Peaches?" The microwave dinged, but he didn't move to get the food.

"Prufrock." Alex sighed. Eventually she was going to have to start talking about her thesis. Might as well start now. "It's about a man at a garden party trying to decide if he should eat a peach."

"The entire poem?"

"He's got dentures and they might slip. It's about regret and lost opportunities."

"In the context of a garden party where they served peaches to a man wearing dentures."

"Yes."

He went into the kitchen and came out with sandwiches and potato salad on two plates. "How long is this poem?"

"A couple of pages, but it's a masterpiece because it focuses on the thoughts of one man, and it's stream of consciousness. My thesis discusses the poem's place in the continuum of development of the individual self in literature."

"Come again?"

"It's a little esoteric."

"No kidding. But the whole poem happens at a tea party."

"Prufrock is at a party, and he thinks all the women there are picking him apart because he's getting older."

"Which is where the peach eating happens. This is not the only thing he's been afraid to try, is it?"

"That's the impression." And also a great insight from someone who hadn't read the poem.

Marc stared at her, and she could see the gears turning. That idiot poem was what led her to break up with Roger. A long spring break spent alone with Prufrock left her nothing to do but think about the isolation she suffered by waiting for Roger. Judging by the expression on Marc's face, it was turning over a few slimy rocks in his head. He didn't fear risk. If his band's gold records on the walls were anything to go by, he'd been successful in a risky business. But something was nagging at him. "I'd like to read that. Can you get me a copy?"

"I have one in my bag upstairs."

"Fantastic."

Alex blinked. That was genuine interest. She'd thought she was prepared for him to be clever, but not for him to be smart. She picked up her plate.

"Where you going?"

"I'm going to warm this up some more."

The bread had not cooled, but he accepted her excuse. He wanted to read Prufrock. It wasn't just about sex. He appeared to like the whole package. Maybe pulling out the Shelley biography wasn't such a bad idea.

"I got the movie in. You wanted to watch it, right?"

She put her sandwich in the microwave for fifteen seconds. The darkness outside seemed to peel away the rest of the world. It was just the two of them here. No past to get in the way. Isolated, but with someone.

* * * *

Marc hit play on the file he'd just recorded. The song sounded dirgy, but it was coming together like butter. And it was the second one this week. The last one had been blindingly hopeful. His phone rang.

"Holy smokes, man, what have you been doing out there?" Jason demanded. "First you send me this song that's like bottled sunshine and Cassie is still walking around the house singing it, and then you send me this melody that's just so—just so lonely. Did she dump you?"

She was lying on the couch reading a book that looked thicker than the Bible.

"So you like them?"

"Like them? Shit, I want to be you when I grow up. She did dump you, didn't she?"

Jason, all the grace of a stampede of buffalo in heat. But the comment about wanting to be him when he grew up? That felt good. "No, she's just introducing me to some things."

Alex glanced up and frowned. Marc shook his head.

"Like what?"

"Just some literature and shit."

"Like the stuff we read in school? Sandy will be so proud."

"Fuck off." Marc grinned. Sandy would be proud.

"Do you want me to try a version of either one and see if I can make any improvements, or do you want to leave them in demo stage?"

"Go ahead and tinker with 'Didn't Know,' but I'm still working on 'Peaches.'"

"What is up with that title anyway? 'Peaches'? Is Paul stuck on a cobbler kick or something?"

Marc smiled. Peaches. "It's temporary."

"Whew, I thought we were going to be laughing your butt out of the writing sessions for it."

Marc laughed and disconnected. Jason wanted to be him when he grew up. Like that was ever going to happen.

"What was that?" Alex asked.

"Just Jason. He got the demos I sent him." Marc grinned again. "He wants to be me when he grows up."

"And this is high praise?"

"Very."

"I'll take your word for that." She went back to her book.

Didn't matter. She also didn't know the difference between a good song and a dud. Over the last blissful day of hanging out with Alex while she worked her way through that tome, he'd worked on five songs. He'd been confident enough about "Peaches" and "Didn't Know" to send them to Jason, but the others were duds that were still on his laptop. She'd said the lyrics sounded a little simple, but otherwise it was all the same to her. That didn't make her any different than any other girlfriend he'd had or most of the non-musicians he'd met. If Jody liked something, it was marketable, but not great songwriting. Cassie had a good ear for a Touchstone song, but couldn't identify which ones sounded better than the others. Maureen had never gone beyond being able to name all the members of Def Leppard and Bon Jovi and listened to NPR like she had when she met Bear. So whether she knew music or not wasn't as important as whether she'd be okay with being alone while he was on tour.

Marc glanced over to where Alex was happily mired in that enormous book. "My buddy Bear's wife was going to the farmer's market with Cassie and Kim." They went every other week so it wasn't a lie. "Maureen helps Kim homeschool her kids."

"Really? Do they live in Potterville, too?" She didn't sound like she'd heard what he had said.

"No, they're in L.A. Everybody lives out there. This is Jason's vacation home."

She nodded, her eyes had not left the book.

"Suzi is working on a new book."

"She writes?"

"Yeah, she writes these amazing horror stories. They're e-books. Our bassist Brian discovered them and bought just about everybody an e-reader so we could read them, too. She writes romance novels, too. Her boyfriend is in Savitar. They're on tour."

"Is that so?" Still engaged in the book.

"She gets bored when he's not home, and she writes a lot to keep herself occupied." Bored? Hell, Suzi got completely crazy. That was something Alex would never have to worry about.

Alex nodded. "That would keep her busy."

His phone rang. Perfect timing. "Hello?"

"Jerry called. He's sleeping with a new one-hit wonder who needs a second hit to keep sleeping with him." Tessa sounded like she was eating a burrito and reading her e-mail. "Jason is writing lullabies full time. Do you have anything?"

Marc scanned his track list. Alex had returned to her book. He was back to square one with her. "I did write this ditty about a short skirt. I didn't think it was going anywhere, but let me rework it to come from a female singer, and I'll send it to him."

"Excellent." Crunch, crunch. "I'll draw up the contract."

"He hasn't bought it yet."

"Like he won't. Come on." She laughed and hung up.

What was that supposed to mean? Not every little scrap of lyrics he sent out sold. Tessa was getting deranged in her old age.

"Maureen has been helping Kim homeschool her kids. She used to be a teacher, but she quit after they were married for a year."

Alex looked up from her book. "What?"

"Bear's wife. She was a teacher."

"And?"

Good question. This topic wasn't going as smoothly as he'd hoped. "Nothing. I was just thinking about them."

"No, that's fine." She closed her book. "I just thought you were mentioning them in passing. Was there something you wanted to discuss? I'm terrible at small talk."

This was worse. Yes, dear, I wanted to find out how you would react to being left alone while I recorded and toured because I don't want to repeat Dez. That would go over great. "I thought you might be getting bored with me working here."

"No, I'm good. I spend a lot of time with a book. You're not bothering me."

Bothering her? Hadn't thought of that. Bothering her. Most women were torn up if he wasn't focused on them all the time. Kind of promising that she could sit there and read just fine with or without him. He opened the file on the short skirts song. He'd been thinking of Alex the night he met her at the diner and ended up fixing the dishwasher. Right now it was a man extolling the virtues of a woman in a short skirt, but it would be easy to retool as a woman extolling the virtues of the same skirt to attract a man. The point of view change would take it from a pervy dud to a cute pop song. Before he was halfway through, his phone rang again.

"Somebody is wearing his big songwriters pants today."

"Ronnie Bauer, to what do I owe the honor?" Marc glanced at Alex. She had to recognize that name. Ronnie was uber-famous. Not knowing Ronnie Bauer was like not knowing Paul McCartney or Steven Spielberg. But she didn't react. She might be as in the dark as Maureen when it came to pop culture.

"Jason forwarded me these new tracks, and they are amazing. I've never heard anything like it from you. Jason said he was going to tinker with them, and I told him I'd break his arms if he touched them."

Marc frowned at the phone. Ronnie Bauer, musical genius, capable of writing a smash hit before breakfast and composing an oratorio between lunch and a nap in the afternoon. "You think they're that good?"

"Peaches" started playing in the background. "You know what this reminds me of? That poem where the beast slouches slowly toward Bethlehem."

"The beast slouches slowly toward Bethlehem?"

Alex perked up. She probably already knew what poem he meant.

"Yeah, the best are, I don't know, tired or something, and the worst are filled with fiery intensity."

"The worst are filled with fiery intensity?"

Alex cocked her head. Now she was paying attention. "'Things fall apart, the center cannot hold. Mere anarchy is loosed upon the world.' 'The Second Coming' by W. B. Yeats."

"That's it!" Ronnie shouted.

Marc almost dropped the phone. Alex smirked at him.

"'Peaches' reminds me of that. You found a smart one. She must be a good influence." Ronnie paused. "You aren't sticking with that title, are you?"

"That's temporary."

"That's good. Listen, my old bandmate Shep wants to do an album, but he's not going to be able to write the material by himself, and I don't have the time right now. Would you be willing to work with him?"

Glen Shepard, most awesome drummer from Star Fury, wanted to do an album and Ronnie Bauer, most awesome all-around musician from Star Fury and a storied solo career, wanted him to help. Marc resisted the desire to drop to his knees chanting, "I'm not worthy." "Are you sure?"

"Christ, man, you've been working with Jason all these years so you have lots of experience molding half-formed ideas, and these new originals of yours are just brilliant. I was mostly concerned about making sure Shep didn't come off like an idiot, but you could give him a respectable solo project."

It was really hard to not fall to his knees. "Jason's a good songwriter on his own."

"Have I or have I not known you boys your entire career? Jason has his moments, but you have always provided polish. I won't lie to you. Shep needs more than polish. Some of the crap he has brought me over the years. I swear he once brought me a song he thought was brilliant and it was a second rate 'Yummy Yummy Yummy.'"

Marc snorted because Ronnie absurdly treated him like an equal and expected him to be cool. "Sure, I can do that. Is there going to be an ego problem?"

"With Shep? If he gets difficult with you, let me know, and I'll kick his ass. I'll tell Shep so his people can get in touch with your people and we can get this ball rolling. Copacetic?"

"Absolutely, and thanks for the opportunity."

"Kid, people give themselves their own opportunities by being ready."

Over twenty years he'd been listening to that. He should believe it by now. "I'll be expecting to hear from Shep."

"You are bailing me out here, and I won't forget it. Enjoy your smart chick. They can get creative in the sack. See ya."

"Bye." Marc clicked off his phone and stared at it, waiting for his heartbeat to slow down.

"You look stunned," Alex said.

"I am. Ronnie wants me to help Glen Shepard write songs for a solo album."

"Surely, you jest."

"Don't call me Shirley." Marc set his guitar in the stand and left the phone on the floor.

"Who is Glen Shepard?" Alex put aside her book.

"He was in Star Fury. They are still one of the top five grossing bands in history, and they broke up forty years ago." He sat down on the couch beside her. Because she had told him about Eliot and had given him that poem to read, he had changed the way he approached songwriting. Because he had changed the way he approached songwriting, Ronnie Bauer had asked him to work on Glen Shepard's solo album.

"So they're good?"

"I'm sure you've heard them. You just might not have realized it." Marc cupped her cheek. Ida and Paul had been more right about her than they knew.

"So this is good news." She bit her lip. Sexy, intelligent, horizon-expanding.

"Excellent news. This is prestigious."

"Congratulations."

Indeed. Ronnie hadn't called Jason to work with Shep. Ronnie hadn't called Marc either until Alex started introducing him to classic literature. Marc kissed her. Dream girl, fantasy gig, and the respect of his peers. Now, he had it all.

Chapter 7

"So how are things going?" Paul asked as he monitored three different meals cooking at the same time. "According to Angela, you've pretty much moved in up the mountain."

"Then you know how things are going." Alex packed half a dozen sausage rolls into a bakery box for a takeout order. That might be the best non-answer she'd ever come up with. Things were great in that they never ran out of conversation topics. Marc had shattered her prejudgment of rock musicians as idiots in half a conversation and kept getting more interesting all the time. When she pulled out the Shelley bio, he'd been curious. And the sex, well, shit, the sex left *her* speechless. He'd also been working on a song, which was fascinating on its own. She'd spent years studying completed and polished works, but she'd never seen a work created. The latest was a complex piece that relied heavily on Prufrock, and another story she'd handed him called *The Chrysanthemums,* which was along the same theme of regret and lost opportunity. She was going to end up influencing a top forty hit with modernist poetry and literature.

On the other hand, things sucked because someday he was going to find out about Roger, and then he'd hate her for being the other woman. Alex jostled the box, scrambling not to drop it.

"Good. Marc is a very nice guy. A bit butch." Paul rolled his eyes. "But there is a certain charm to the manly man."

"I suppose." The tone was too cool, but it slipped out before she caught herself.

Paul lost interest in the food he was cooking to focus on her. "What do you mean by that?"

"Nothing." She slid the bakery box into a plastic bag. "I've got a table waiting for those dinners. Don't burn them."

Paul made a derisive noise. "You are talking to the only Michelin-rated short order cook on the planet."

"You are not Michelin-rated."

"I can dream."

Drew pushed through the door.

"Yes, I can see it now. The *Michelin Guide to West Virginia*," Alex said, heading out.

"More like the *Goodyear Guide to West Virginia*." Drew clipped his orders to the line. "Alex, there's a guy asking for you. He sat down in my section so I reseated him in yours."

"Marc?"

"No. Different guy."

Alex blinked as the information coalesced in her brain. Oh, no. She stumbled down the steps in her effort to get out. She dropped off the sausage rolls and the bill without saying anything to the customers. "What are you doing here?" she hissed at Roger. Drew had at least put him at the very edge of her section, nearly on the sidewalk. He belonged on the curb where she'd kicked him months ago.

"I needed to talk to you, and this is the only place I can ever find you." The circles under his eyes gave him a hound dog air. The shirt he wore had ketchup on the sleeve, but since Carla wasn't here to take care of him, he probably had no clean laundry.

"You could email me like professionals do, because that's all we are. Professional co-workers."

"We were more. We can be more again."

Funny how his allure wasn't working so well now. She had Marc to thank for that. "No, we really can't." Alex put her hands on her hips. "You need to order something if you're going to stay here."

"Alex, if you'll just listen to me, I can fix this. I love you."

"Yes, well, we all want stuff we can't have. Coffee?"

"Alex, please, come to my cabin later so we can talk. You're being foolish."

"Roger, you're still my advisor, and we have to work together until I finish my thesis. Let's just try to be mature about it. Unless you want me to request a new advisor and explain why to the dean." Alex took a step back from the table. "I'll get that coffee."

Roger grabbed her wrist, pulling her back toward him. "No, you have to listen to me."

"No, I don't." Alex tried to twist free, but failed. Symbolic, no? "You need to let me go or you're going to be in deep shit."

"You're already in deep shit, buddy. Hands off." Marc stepped between them breaking Roger's grip. "You need to leave."

Alex staggered backward remembering how Marc had looked like he was about to commit a felony when she walked up to his table the first time. Now he not only looked capable, but like he had planned it and was ready to execute. She glanced toward the diner. Ida stood on the sidewalk with the portable phone in her hand. Paul was at the out door from the kitchen, wiping his hands on the towel he kept draped over his shoulder all the time. Drew and Tina were at the outside drink station, suspended in the act of filling drinks. Every one of the diners had stopped eating. The cavalry had arrived and everybody was watching.

"This is a private matter." Roger stood up. The altitude didn't help him any. His full doughy mass was at least half a foot shorter than Marc.

"And this is a private establishment where we don't tolerate that shit." Marc wasn't touching Roger, but the force of his anger was electric.

Alex shuffled back into their radius. She needed to defuse this before Roger said something unfortunate, and Marc found out the truth before she was ready. "Marc, I can handle this."

"It's already handled. Go on inside. This guy's leaving."

Alex's jaw tightened. He just told her to go inside. Like she was his to order around. Who died and made him emperor of her soul? "Excuse me? I can handle this myself."

Marc glared at her, and for a second she imagined that she saw the realization that he'd overstepped. "He's leaving, anyway." Marc turned back to Roger. "Aren't you?"

"Alex, I'll speak with you later." Roger stormed away.

Marc turned around. That awareness she'd seen earlier was definitely there now. "He knows you."

"If you'd given me a second before swooping in like an avenging angel, I could have told you that."

"He looked like he was getting handsy with you."

If he only knew. Then again, if he did know, it would all be up in smoke. A man who valued honesty in relationships was never going to want to be with some other man's other woman. Alex folded her arms. "I had it under control."

"Hey, kids." Ida broke in. "You know I called Junie Keyes, and she'd love to get in a few extra hours, so she's going to come in and cover the rest of your shift, Alex. Why don't you just head home?"

Home. She'd been planning on heading up the mountain with Marc for the afternoon and evening. A temporary liaison. She'd been crashing at Angela and Finn's for the summer, not really home. Her dorm room at school was only home for the duration of her college career. When she left for school, her mother had made over her old bedroom as a scrapbooking room and when Alex visited they opened up the sleeper chair for her. She had no home.

She should have stuck with her burqa and celibacy plan.

"Fine." Alex bashed into the kitchen through the out door. Paul didn't make a peep about it. She tossed her apron in the hamper and grabbed her purse out of her locker. "You tell whoever takes over my section that I get the tips."

"You know Marc didn't mean any harm," Paul said.

"I don't care what Marc meant. It was none of his goddamn business." And if he found out the truth, he was going to hate her. That would hurt more than anything.

"Alex," Marc said through the screen. "Come on. Let's go home so we can talk."

"I planned on going home, but not with you." She shoved out through the in door, nearly smacking him in the face with it.

Marc caught her arm as she passed him. "Alex, please. Everyone is staring."

"Aren't you doing exactly what you just kicked someone out of the restaurant for doing? It's not even your restaurant."

Marc looked at where his long fingers wrapped around her forearm before he released her. "Fair enough, but I still want to talk to you."

"So did he, before you threatened to beat him up."

"I never threatened him. I told him to leave you alone, and I have twenty witnesses to attest to it."

"My God, you're self-centered."

Marc squeezed his eyes shut and shook his head. "What? Where did that even come from?"

"How can you be worried about having witnesses now?"

"Because people sue celebrities all the time. Can we please just have a private conversation?" He put his hand on her shoulder and leaned in so she could hear his lowered voice. "Look, I'm sorry if I butted in. I was concerned about you. That guy looked like he wanted to hurt you. Surely, you can see that."

Roger? Hurt her? Yes, but not physically.

Marc chewed the inside of his cheek. She'd missed her part of their joke, and it bugged him. That had to mean something. "I was trying to protect you. I love you, and I didn't want to see you hurt. Now, can we please finish this conversation someplace where we don't have an audience?"

Alex scanned the seating area. Plenty of diners were tuned in to the drama as they ate. If she went back to Angela and Finn's, she wouldn't have to worry about what would happen if Marc ever found out about her adulteress status, and she could focus all her energy on worrying about what Roger was going to do next. But that wasn't much in the spirit of "The Love Song of Alfred J. Prufrock."

Wait. "What did you say?"

"I want to finish this conversation away from the spotlight."

"Before that."

"I didn't want to see you hurt. The way he had your arm, I thought he was going to twist it off." Marc frowned, his eyes darting to the sides as if he could see the diners watching them through the back of his head.

"No, before that."

He straightened and heaved a sigh. "Alex, please can we go someplace private?"

"I swear you said you loved me."

"I did," he said through his teeth.

"But you won't say it again now, so how do I know you meant it?" If he loved her, that changed things. He might even be willing to forgive her tawdry past.

"You are killing me here, Alex."

"Why can't you just say it?"

Marc turned his head to meet the astonished gaze of the woman at the table next to them.

"Tell her," the woman said.

"Oh, God," Marc groaned. "This is going to be all over the Internet."

"I'm recording it," a woman at the table next to the drink station said. She had her phone in her hand. "I recorded it the first time, too."

"Oh, good," her dinner companion said. "I'm going to want to watch that over and over. This is history."

These people were far too fascinated with what should be a personal moment. So he was a musician. His love life should have no impact on his ability to play guitar. On the other hand, if he said it now, in front of all these people, he must mean it, right? People, total strangers were recording it for posterity. Roger wouldn't look her in the eye in class. He hadn't wanted anyone to get an inkling of what was going on behind his closed office door. Some people in the English department believed he disliked her because of the way he acted toward her in public. If Marc went on the Internet on video saying that he loved her, then everyone would know.

Yeah, she was going to be one of those women who made their man prove he loved her.

"Alex, I love you."

The seven tables closest to them broke into applause.

"Can we please finish this in private?" He held out his hand.

Alex blinked back tears. He loved her, publicly and on video. She slid her hand into his and let him pull her out so their audience could see them. He took a deep bow, creating more applause, before escorting her to his car.

"You love me?" she asked as he held the door open for her.

"Yes." He kissed her nose. "Get in the car."

"Surely, you don't mean it."

"Don't call me Shirley."

* * * *

Alex closed her eyes as the door clicked closed behind them. He had said he loved her and there was no reason for him to lie. She put her hands on his cheeks. They were rough with stubble and so warm and real. "You love me?"

He leaned in to kiss her. She closed her eyes when his warm lips touched hers. Every moment she spent with him, he made her feel like the center of the universe. The desperate longing to be with him every second nearly destroyed her. What was she going to do when he left her? He would. He'd find out and move on. There had to be something she could do to keep that from happening.

Alex pulled her shirt off. "I want you."

"You know you don't have to put out every time I look at you."

She shimmied out of her jeans and stretched out on the rug in front of the fireplace. "Even if I want to?"

"Bad girl."

Her breath hitched. No, he meant that as a compliment. "But only in the right places."

He crawled over her. The scent of his heated skin made her crazy. Would he notice if she stole one of his shirts so she could have it forever? The scent coming from him and the smell of him on her flesh. It was delicious. Her skin pinched and puckered at the thought. He trailed kisses down her neck and between her breasts. "I want to wrap you up and take you home."

"I didn't know I was on the menu."

"You were on mine." He traced one of her nipples with the tip of his tongue.

She gasped, arching.

"You're the best thing that's ever happened to me," he murmured, his breath brushing over her skin.

Writhing, she moaned, trying to release some of the tension building inside her. "That feels so good. I wish I could please you as much as you please me."

"You do." He trailed farther down her body.

"The way your mouth feels…" Her words were lost in a pleasured sigh as he kissed the crease at the top of her thigh. "Oh, Marc." Alex dug her fingers into the carpet, helpless as his confident hands spread her legs. Her muscles shivered like over tightened strings. His fingers ran up the back of her thigh to her knee. His fingers stayed there, nestled in the crook behind her knee. When she opened her eyes, he was sitting between her legs, studying her. Articulating a thought took too much effort. Instead, she reached for him.

Smiling, he stretched out on top of her, angling his leg under her thigh to spread her wider. She clenched her teeth, burying her hands in his hair as he kissed her. The rough material of his shirt rubbed her tender nipples until she shuddered. Nothing was like this. Nothing had ever been like this. She wrapped her legs around his lean hips, desperate to be connected to him. "Please, please," she whispered.

He started riding against her. Through his jeans, she could feel his cock straining. "This works better without pants," he gasped.

She laughed breathlessly.

He got back up on his knees and pulled off his shirt before reaching for his jeans. "I had planned to tease you a little more. I underestimated you." He pushed down his jeans and fell on her, thrusting.

Alex held her breath to keep from crying out when he buried himself inside her. She was lost to the endless rhythm of their bodies working together. Half smothering herself, she held back her own delighted cries. She could only hold on, letting him take her wherever he wanted until he found her shattering point. He shuddered and groaned a moment later. Afterward, he rolled onto his side, cuddling her close.

He was here, and he had said he loved her. Unfortunately, the second he found out about Roger, she was out. Losing Marc was the price of that horrible error in judgment. If there was just some way to explain it to him so he wouldn't hate her. Right now, the only option she could come up with was to walk away at the end of the summer and leave a note, confessing what a mistake she'd made getting involved with Roger. "It's been a really long day."

"Go to sleep, my darling." He kissed her forehead. "You're right where you belong again."

"Where's that?"

"In my arms."

* * * *

Marc woke up with a shaft of sunlight boring through his eyelids. Alex was curled into his side with one hand over her face, shielding her eyes, but she stirred as soon as he moved. "Good morning, beautiful," he said.

"I'm pretty sure it's late afternoon, early evening."

"Kinda feels like a brand new day to me." He ran his tongue over his teeth. So much like a brand new day that he wanted to brush, floss, and have a bowl of cereal.

She laughed and sat up. "What a day."

Marc ran his fingers down her spine making her look at him over her shoulder. "I never want to be without you."

A slight frown creased her brow for a moment before it was gone. "What?"

He sat up and took her hands. "I never want to be without you." When he leaned in and kissed her, she didn't respond. "Alex?"

"I think I missed something."

"I want you to move in with me. Or me to move in with you. I could get a place near your school until you finish your degree. Or forever if you wanted. I can live about anywhere. Music takes me away from home a lot, so you would have lots of time to work on your studies."

That frown creased her brow again, lingering this time. "I don't know."

"I know this was supposed to be a summer thing, but I've never felt this before. When Bear met Maureen, I thought he was being a sucker. I had no idea what it was like to really fall in love."

"Weren't you married?"

"I know!" Jeez, Dez. He'd been a complete idiot marrying her. That was a kiddie pool. This was Olympic-pool size. Deep and wide and exactly the right temperature. He couldn't explain that to her. It sounded stupid in his head. She'd think he'd lost his marbles.

"We just met."

"Joseph Campbell said marriage is a recognition of spiritual identity. I recognized me in you and you in me the moment I met you." Something in his chest slid into place. Life with Alex. Home was wherever she was.

"Marriage." Alex pulled back. She scrambled off the bed. "Why are you talking about marriage?"

"Don't panic. This is right." Marc stood in front of her and put his hands on her shoulders. The sun was behind her, giving her a halo, but she was shaking so hard he should have been able to hear the vibration. "Alex, I want to treat you like a precious stone. Let me."

"Let you?" she whispered. "I'm afraid. What if you fi—fall out of love with me?"

"It won't happen. You will never have to be alone."

Alex sucked in a deep breath like a drowning woman who had just been pulled onto the beach. "No matter what?"

"There is nothing that would drive me away from you."

She pulled back, blinking. "Nothing?"

"Alex, I wish I could explain to you how I feel, but I can't. There are no words." He gathered her hands into his. Her delicate, wonderful hands. "I never want to be without you, and I know it's going to be hard, and I know there's going to be times when we can't be together, but I want to spend every second I can of the rest of my life with you."

She blinked. "Every second?"

"Every second."

"For the rest of your life?"

"Absolutely."

"No matter what?"

"No matter what you do."

Sobbing, she sunk into his arms. Not the response he expected, but it worked.

* * * *

"I think you're nuts," Marc said, pulling the car into park in front of Angela and Finn's.

"I might be, but I have the opening shift and I can't let Ida and Paul down."

"So put in your notice tomorrow. Tell them you have a full-time job being in love with me." He pulled her hand to his lips.

Alex shivered. He'd promised and meant it. At least, he meant it now.

But Marc, something about the way he stammered over his words, made it seem too true for speech. It reminded her of the Mathew Arnold poem that said something about love being too weak to unlock the heart and let it speak. "I made a commitment, and I want to keep it."

"Okay, but I think you're going to regret every minute you're not with me." He drew a deep breath with his eyes fixed on hers. "I know I'm going to regret every minute you're not with me."

"No wonder you're such a successful songwriter."

He chuckled and released her hand. "I'll see you tomorrow bright and early."

"No. Don't you dare come in until the end of my shift, or I'll never get any work done. Ida will kill you."

"Fine. I'll be there tomorrow, and we can start planning that big trip to Italy you always dreamed of."

Italy. Last night when he had suggested delaying her master's for a semester to travel to Italy with him, it had taken all of ten seconds for her to agree. He loved her. Three months traveling through Italy with Marc and away from Roger. The master's program would be there when she was ready, and by that time, maybe Roger would have gotten himself together so she wouldn't have to worry about the two of them bumping into one another. The loans would have to be dealt with when the time came. She leaned in and pecked him on the cheek before jumping out of the car. Anymore than that, and she might never get into the house. "Bye."

"See you tomorrow."

He waited on the street until she closed the front door behind her. She leaned on it, sighing, listening to the car pull away. Angela and Finn both turned away from tonight's crime dramedy to look at her.

"Well?" Angela asked.

"He wants me to move in with him. He's taking me to Italy."

Finn snorted and turned back to the TV, but Angela jumped up. "Really? Italy? What about school?"

"I'm going to delay it. He said they're not going into the studio for a while so we can spend the time together. I might even transfer to UCLA to finish up. If I finish at all."

"If? You'd quit?"

"He mentioned marriage."

"Marriage!" Angela threw her arms around Alex. "I knew it. I just knew it. You two are perfect for each other."

"I guess so." Alex pulled away and rubbed her face. "I have to clean up and get to bed. I open in the morning. Good night."

After a quick shower, she opened her e-mail. The first one was from the university congratulating her on finishing her master's thesis, and if she had any questions "do not reply to this e-mail address, but contact your advisor." Master's thesis, she hadn't… The time on the e-mail said it had arrived about an hour and a half after she and Marc had left the diner. She opened her sent e-mail. About the time Marc was declaring his undying devotion, she had snuck home and submitted a master's thesis and had been back in time to sink sobbing into Marc's arms.

Roger. That bastard.

Yanking on a T-shirt and a pair of jeans, she ran out to the living room where Angela and Finn were still planted in front of the television. "I need to borrow your car."

"Okay." Angela stood up.

"Why?" Finn asked. That made Angela stop. If he'd kept his mouth shut, she'd have the keys in her hands by now.

Alex dug her fingernails into her palms. *Well, Finn, I have to go beg my ex-lover to get a paper back before he ruins any hope I have of an academic career.* "I need to go up the mountain."

Angela crossed the room to her purse and rummaged for a minute to find the keys before holding them out.

Alex ran out the door and jumped in Angela's gold Taurus. She reversed out of the driveway, flinging gravel and no doubt upsetting Finn. Roger couldn't do this. This wasn't the action of a man in love. This was crazy. Alex had to go slower than she wanted once she reached the mountain because the road dropped off right behind the barrier. One wrong move and she'd go flying into the trees like she was starring in a summer blockbuster movie. That was pretty symbolic, too. One wrong move, and her life was over. At the campground, she slowed to a crawl, letting the headlights sweep around the circle of cabins. Roger's car was parked in front of one at the back. She pulled in behind him. Ignoring the stares of the couple sitting on their porch watching a bunch of kids chase fireflies in the middle of the circle of cabins, she banged on the door.

"Alex." Roger smiled like it was Christmas morning. "I knew you would come. Come inside."

"You knew I would come? How could I not? What are you doing?" Alex snarled. Her throat ached from not screaming. She should be screaming.

Roger looked over her shoulder at the couple next door. "Inside."

Alex stepped in. She could hash it out with Marc in the middle of dinner rush, and she couldn't with Roger when there were only two witnesses. Very telling. The small living room had a neat pile of books on the table next to the laptop. Positioned as if they had just been unpacked. "Roger, what are you trying to do to me?"

"I told you. I've submitted your thesis. I knew you wouldn't want to do it yourself." He reached for her. "What is it?"

"Of course I wouldn't want to do it myself. It wasn't my thesis. I can't steal someone else's work. Especially Melanie's. She's dead. That's so wrong. It's not even plagiarism. It's grave robbing."

"Alex, you are working with antiquated ideas of right and wrong. It's so charmingly feminine of you."

Charmingly feminine. He said it all the time. His way of saying that she was a stupid woman. Her time in the mountains with Marc was doing some good. "Roger—"

"Listen to me, my dear. From a certain perspective, this is right." He was smiling ever so slightly, but smiling just the same. Unbelievable.

Alex opened her mouth, but nothing came out. Her brain had slammed to a stop so fast she thought inertia must have carried it forward into her skull causing a concussion. "From a certain perspective? Are you mad?"

"You were writing a paper about lost opportunity, and you were losing an opportunity. This thesis was nearly finished. I polished it a little for you as a thank you for all the work you've done for me all these years and for the depth of our relationship. To prove that I love you."

"Wait. Let me get this straight." Alex pressed her hands over her temples hoping that would keep her brain from slamming to a stop again. "You submitted a stolen thesis from my e-mail address. You hacked into my e-mail account to send a stolen thesis. A thesis stolen from a dead girl. And somehow you think this is okay? This is the right thing to do?"

"Alex, you're repeating yourself." Roger tried to put his arm around her again, but she dodged him.

"That's because I can't believe it. I keep hearing it over and over in my head and with every repetition, it gets more tawdry and reprehensible."

"You know I would do anything for you. You are like a siren, and I have crashed myself on your rocks."

Alex rubbed her face. "Greek mythology? Really?"

"You lured me in, Alex. You knew I was unhappy with my wife." He shook his head, like he was forgiving her for a youthful mistake.

"I did?"

"You were so lovely and so attentive. The worthy little helpmate. Sometimes a little naive, but I find that so attractive in a woman. When I met you in class, you knew what I needed before I asked." Roger brushed her hair off her cheek. "How could I have resisted you when I could see how hard you were trying to please me? You brought me coffee, just the way I liked it every class that term."

"Not every class." Every class after the first week. She'd been headed to lunch that Tuesday in September and saw him in the hall, looking like he hadn't slept in days. She'd already been nursing a ferocious crush on the clever, gentle professor and wanted to do something for him. On the way to his class, she'd picked up a cappuccino—no foam, double sugar—

because she remembered him saying that he liked it that way. Was that all it took? "Cappuccino drinkers are warmhearted but can be absent minded. No foam because you'd end up looking silly."

"And double sweet because I have terrible impulse control. You reinvented yourself as the perfect woman for me so I would fall in love with you and cheat on my wife." He stroked her cheek. "You saved me from a joyless existence."

When she had ice cream with Marc on the town square, she'd been very curious about what flavor he chose because it was a reflection of his personality. She'd researched him online and dressed to please him. Her whole plan after the first day they met was to reinvent herself as Marc's perfect woman. Was that all love was? One person who was so desirable that someone else rearranged their entire personality to please them?

"You wanted me to fall in love with you, and now you're going to punish me by leaving me. You can't leave me." He clasped his hands in front of his chest. "I can't let you go."

"I never meant to lure you away from your wife." Or had she? It had been so long ago. He had been the very attractive, scholarly Brit Lit professor with the tweed coat and the brown leather briefcase. She'd been crazy about him. Had she lured him away from Carla?

"I need you, Alex. Please don't leave me."

Marc was here on this same mountain. He had told he loved her, too. He had said he wanted to take her away to Italy and marry her. But when he found out she had tricked him into falling in love with her, that was going to change. She wasn't any better than his ex-wife. "I have to go."

"Meet me at the university. In my office. We'll straighten this all out, my darling. No more of this silliness."

"Yes." Alex blinked. Marc had called her his darling, too. "Your office. I have to go."

On the way down the mountain, Alex contemplated hitting the gas instead of the brakes and letting the car fly off the side of the mountain. The cursed thesis. Killed the writer and the thief.

"I have to go home. I need a ride to the bus station," Alex announced when she walked in the door.

Finn stepped out of the bathroom with toothpaste foaming out of his mouth, wearing blue striped pajamas. "What?"

"I have to go to the bus station now. I need to go home." Alex walked past him to her room and started jamming her things in her suitcase. All this time she'd been thinking she was the Typhoid Mary of marriage when she was the much more culpable Mata Hari.

"What do you mean you have to go now? Right now?" Angela asked from the doorway.

"Do you know what time it is?" Finn demanded.

"I have to go right now!" Alex screamed.

"What happened?" Angela asked.

Alex slammed her suitcase closed. A sleeve dangled out the side. Tears started to stream down her face. She had manipulated Roger. She'd made herself into his perfect woman and pursued him until he gave in. Then she'd left him high and dry. No wonder he came after her. She was foolish and feminine, a stupid little girl. "I have to go."

"Alex." Angela tried to hug her, but Alex pushed her away. Angela stumbled into the dresser, shocked.

"Hey!" Finn shouted, grabbing for Angela as if she might fall. "You are not getting violent with my wife in my house."

"Then take me to the bus station. I have to leave. I can't stay here."

"All right, hold your horses while I get some pants on." Finn went to their bedroom.

"Alex, I don't understand. Did something happen between you and Marc? You were so happy before."

Happy. When she thought she could escape her mistakes, but she was making them all over again. She was tricking another man into loving her. She couldn't abandon Roger after all he'd done for her.

Unless she could stop it. She could bear the guilt of nearly taking Roger away from his family, but not stealing a thesis, too. Somehow she needed to stop that mess. Roger had meant well. He really had, but that was wrong on top of wrong.

Marc was better off without her. The last thing he needed in his life was another woman using him. He didn't deserve that.

She had never deserved him.

Chapter 8

Marc walked into the diner whistling. He'd wrapped up "Peaches" this morning and short of a title, it was pretty well done. Tessa e-mailed to ask him if he wanted the contract for the "Short Skirts" song sent FedEx, or if he'd be in L.A. within the next month to sign them in the office. Shep had called, and in a drug-addled way, had offered to let him work on his upcoming solo project, followed by a thanks for helping him out. Working with Shep might be prestigious, but it was looking like it might be even more trying than working with Jason. At least Jason was clean and sober. Now he was starved and desperate for some Alex.

The diner was full. In fact, a little more full than usual, and Junie's mom was waiting tables. Ida glared up from where she was taking an order. Why was Ida taking orders?

"You. Sit. I need to talk to you," she barked.

Marc pointed at his chest.

"Don't play dense," Ida snapped and pointed at the stool behind the register with a hot pink talon.

Marc took another look around the diner. No Alex. Perching on the stool, he checked outside. No Alex. She said she had opening duty this morning. That was why she wanted to go back to Angela and Finn's yesterday evening. She would be off the clock in about twenty minutes, but unless she was in the bathroom, she wasn't here. Paul was glaring at him through the service window.

"What did you do to that poor little girl?" Ida marched toward the register and Marc swore the floor trembled like a herd of *T. rexes* were approaching instead of a single late middle-aged woman.

"Where's Alex?" Marc asked.

"She went back to school." Ida started tapping her talons on the counter. The sound was loud enough to echo through the diner.

"Why?"

"Well, that is the million dollar question, isn't it? We want to know what happened between you two after you left here yesterday."

That was hardly a story he was going to tell, not in any detail. "Let's continue this in the kitchen."

"Let's do it right damn now."

Marc frowned at Ida. She liked to give a good show, but this was ridiculous. Then he noticed the set of her mouth and that she still had the order she'd just taken in her hand. Ida wasn't putting on a show, she was livid.

"In the kitchen." Marc pushed passed her. Everyone in the diner watched them walk through the door so Marc kept going to the storage area. Paul called Junie's mother to cover him. The way they ran this place sometimes, he was surprised they ever got any business. "Now, what happened?"

"That's what we want to know," Paul said.

Fight at restaurant. Make up. Crazy great sex. Soulful conversation. Asked her to move in with him. Alluded to marriage. Convinced her to take a semester off and go to Italy. Discussed her summer job and how she couldn't just quit because they needed her.

In retrospect, that was rich.

"I dropped her off last night because she said she was opening this morning."

"And what happened when she went back up the mountain?" Paul folded his arms over his filthy apron. Bad morning all around if Paul had gotten that much food on himself.

"She didn't. At least I didn't see her. I dropped her off and planned to pick her up about now. What did Angela say?"

Ida touched her hair in that nervous gesture she used when things weren't working the way she wanted them to or when she was flirting. She wasn't flirting. "When Alex didn't show this morning, we called over. Angela said you dropped her off last night and about a half hour later she came tearing out of her room wanting to borrow the car. She went up the mountain and was gone maybe half an hour before she came back and demanded to be taken to the bus station so she could go back to school."

Marc scratched his head. "I don't know what happened. I'll see if I can reach her." He walked out feeling like there was a white-hot spotlight on his head. In the car, he called her but wasn't surprised when there was no answer.

To text or not to text.

She could only be running away from him. The last thing he wanted was to end up as a Twitterverse wonder because she posted a screen shot of his pathetic attempt to contact her. Poor Marc Wells, chasing a woman who was too young for him like a washed up old man who was never very talented in the first place. Next stop, a reality show with Andrew Ridgely, John Oates, and Art Garfunkel.

Marc swallowed and slid the phone in his pocket.

He was supposed to be the guy in the band with his shit together. Ty was the charismatic one. Jason was the artist. Brian was the friendly one. Bear used to be the fun one, but since he married Maureen, he'd become the romantic one. Marc had always been the strong, responsible one. The one who read the contracts, made the connections, and didn't screw up.

Who had just fallen flat on his face over a woman. A woman too young for him. The band was going to give him shit about this for years. If the tabloids got ahold if it, Twitter would be the least of his worries. They'd hunt down every girl he'd ever dated for comments. Dez would have no money worries for a while because she'd demand top dollar for her insight as his ex-wife. He was going to be publically humiliated on every channel.

The only feasible plan was to pretend like Alex didn't mean that much to him. A little summer lovin'. Go home to California where he could make himself busy and hope Alex's magic touch hadn't worn off. Ronnie was depending on him to keep Shep from looking ridiculous, and if he failed, he'd never get another chance like this again. He'd spend the rest of his life as the other guitarist in Touchstone.

* * * *

Alex opened up her dorm room. Fucking elevators. Who closed both elevators at the same time for maintenance in a ten-story building? People who thought no one would be in the building, that was who.

All the way here, she'd been looking back down the road, half fearing, half hoping to see Marc's car chasing down the bus. She'd imagined him stopping the bus and carrying her off, promising to fix everything. Convince the dean that she had nothing to do with the thesis Roger submitted in her name. Tell her he didn't care that she'd pursued a married man. That it was Roger's choice, too. And that he still loved her. Most importantly, that he still loved her. Marc could do that. He'd waded into the utter disaster at the diner and fixed it all. If he could do that, he could make all this go away.

Like that was going to happen. Roger was right. She'd made herself into a siren, designed for him, and lured him away from his wife. Now he had to keep her by whatever means necessary, even if it meant the destruction of her career.

And causing her to lose Marc.

Not that Roger cared about that. As long as he had what he wanted, he didn't care about the aftermath. She'd been blind to never notice that before. He wanted to be worshipped. Someone to bring him coffee, write his papers, and play captive audience to his tragic story. All this time she'd believed he loved her. Fool didn't even cover what she was. In the next few days, she needed to get the smarts to extricate herself from this mess.

Not that she'd been planning on the relationship with Marc going anywhere. If he hadn't thrown her out the moment she told him the truth, it would have grated between them like sand in an oyster shell. In an oyster that became a pearl, but between people, it could only be a festering wound. And if she had to tell him the whole truth? The ice cream analyzing, Googling, short skirt and high heels wearing sham she'd created to lure him into her clutches?

Nothing short of disaster. Complete, humiliating disaster.

The whole thing had nearly come unraveled last week at the diner.

Not last week. Two days ago. Alex sat down on her unmade bed and rested her forehead on her knees. Two days ago.

A soft knock interrupted Alex before she dissolved. Her shirt had ridden up her back so she jerked her it back into place, hoping the act would pull her brain back together, too. It didn't. Neither did the pause to check her face in the mirror on the way to the door.

Cheryl, the resident director, stood outside with her usual pleasant smile. "Hey, Alex, I thought I— What happened?" She stepped inside, closing the door behind her as if there were anybody in the entire building to eavesdrop. "Alex, what happened?"

"Bad romance." That summed it up well enough.

"Honey, are you sure? You look like the world ended some time yesterday. Do you want to talk about it?" Cheryl put her hand up in anticipation of Alex's protest. "I know you like to keep to yourself, but it's just the two of us in this big old building."

"I don't want to talk about it."

"All right. I just noticed that you'd come back early. The elevators are going to be out for at least a week so you're going to be hoofing it up and down the stairs if you plan to stay here."

"That's fine. I like the idea of starving in my garret. Maybe I'll get my thesis done before classes start."

Cheryl frowned. "I thought you were done with that."

Shit. Shit! Did the whole world know? "How did you know?"

"I had lunch with Gerald Vukovich yesterday. He said he was surprised you invited him to be on your master's committee. He thought you were doing Eliot."

Gerald Vukovich? Roger was putting together her thesis committee? She needed to get into her e-mail and find out what else he'd done in her name. Oh, and change her password so he couldn't do it again. "Things have been a little crazy this summer. That's why I had to come back. Right now, I'm on a bit of a deadline. Can I catch up with you later?" Alex maneuvered Cheryl back toward the door and pulled it open.

"I bet you are on a deadline trying to get that dissertation defended by the end of the third summer session." Cheryl leaned on the door jamb. She wasn't known as Captain Oblivious for nothing. The woman could not take a hint spelled out in twenty-foot tall burning letters in the middle of the student center.

"I'd love to chat, but let me get situated, and I'll drop in on you later today. Okay?" Alex closed the door in Cheryl's face. She heard Cheryl jump back. Well, those who had no clue when to take a hint sometimes had to get a door in the face.

Alex turned to her desk. Since she was the returning floor supervisor, she hadn't had to empty her room like most people, but nothing had been updated since her life started falling apart around spring break. The calendar still read April. Her syllabi had either fallen off the wall or were hanging by dried-up tape. Old papers littered the floor. It might have been better if they'd made her clear out her room. She set her laptop on a pile of papers and opened it.

According to her sent mail, Roger had submitted the Plath thesis to the university shortly after Marc ordered him out of the diner for grabbing her. By the time they were at his house making love, Roger had been sequestered in his cabin at the campground next door, polishing the paper, hacking her e-mail, and submitting it.

Damn it, she hadn't changed the password yet. She veered into the settings and created a password that looked more like cartoon physicists swearing than English.

Back in sent mail, she found e-mails written, which sounded eerily like her, to six professors including Vukovich, asking them to be in her thesis committee. None of them were Plath scholars except Diana Gregor, who had been Melanie's advisor. Which begged the question, what did

Roger have on Dr. Gregor? Not that Alex needed to know, but it did add to Roger's image of a bottom-feeding bloodsucker.

What had she been thinking in chasing him? He'd appeared to be so intelligent and wounded, trapped in his unhappy marriage. She'd just wanted to make him happy. Which she had done too successfully based on the way he was pursuing her now.

In her inbox, she found that Dr. Gregor had accepted within an hour of the invitation, and three others had accepted since. The senile Dr. Whittier had asked in a moment of lucidity why she wanted him on a committee for a Plath thesis when he was a Norse scholar, and she'd never had a class with him. His e-mail signature looked like it could have been created with sticks, and she hoped it wasn't some kind of Norse curse. She had no answer for him. She guessed Roger had chosen him to add gravitas to her committee since he was the oldest professor on campus and very respected in his unrelated field. She only needed four. And the four who had accepted were either easygoing types who would have approved her thesis if it had been written in crayon on a freshly painted wall, or in the case of Dr. Gregor, were probably being blackmailed by Roger.

She grabbed the phone off the wall and dialed Roger's house. He'd be home by now, waiting to meet with her in his office where they could "straighten all this out, darling."

"Hello?"

"How could you?"

"Alex! Where are you?" He sounded so relieved that it broke her heart a little. He really loved her even if he had to ruin her life to show it.

"In hell as far as I can tell. Although I'm not sure if it would be in the circle for adulterers or the circle for liars and cheats. If they were next door, maybe I could shift back and forth."

"What are you talking about?"

"The committee. The thesis committee!"

"But it's for you, my love. Vukovich is so honored to be asked, he'll give you a pass. Anders has always felt if you did the work to get this far, then the thesis was just a formality. Lucci thinks publish or perish is a crock and will approve any old thing to undermine it."

"And Dr. Gregor?"

"She's going to give you credibility. She owes me a favor, and if she gives you a thumbs up, you're in for any teaching position in the country."

"Where they are going to expect me to be a Sylvia Plath scholar." Alex pounded her fist against the wall. "I don't know anything about Sylvia Plath other than she wrote *The Bell Jar* and stuck her head in an oven."

"So for your doctorate, you'll stay here and return to the Modernists because they are your first love. This is all academic."

Had he just said it was academic to mean it was inconsequential? It wasn't inconsequential. It was her life, and it *was* academic. This was impossible.

"Honestly, honey, your defense is going to be eight hours of talking about the weather with a break for lunch, and at the end you're going to have a job. I haven't told you the best part."

"Best?" When would this nightmare end?

"I talked to HR and you could have freshman English classes starting fall semester."

"Roger. You can't do this."

"Do what?"

"This is cheating. It's plagiarism. I didn't write that thesis. I didn't earn this."

"Alex, most people would be thrilled. I've ensured your entire career."

"Ensured? You have me chained to you for the rest of my life. I can't leave this university unless I buckle down and learn everything there is to know about Sylvia Plath, and I'd rather stick my head in an oven. If any of this ever came out, I would be ruined."

"I thought you wanted to be with me. You said you loved me. When the time was right, I was going to leave Carla so we could be together."

Alex twisted her hands together. She had said those things, and at the time, she'd believed them, but now she knew it wasn't love she had had felt for Roger because love was what Marc had shown her. Mentioning Marc would make Roger go unhinged, and she needed him at least practicing sane for the moment. "I don't want you to leave Carla for me. I just want you to be happy."

"You make me happy. I can't live without you."

"You have been living without me. I went away, and you survived just fine."

"When you left, you proved to me that I needed to work harder to keep you. I made it so—"

Alex jumped up, knocking over her chair. "You made it so I was beholden to you for the rest of my life. How could you? I thought you loved me, but you never did, did you? You just wanted someone to worship you and need you." Marc had lots of people to worship him. That was the last thing he wanted in a relationship. Of course, being stupid with Roger had precluded being happy with Marc. A sob caught in her throat. "Have you even tried to work things out with Carla?"

"Alex, I never meant to hurt you."

She laughed. It grated in her chest more like broken glass than joy. "What am I supposed to do, Roger?"

"Stay with me. You'll get your doctorate and settle into a nice teaching position. And when the baby starts school, I'll be able to leave Carla. I promise this time. I am going to leave her."

"Surely, you are." *Don't call me Shirley.*

"You can't leave me. I can ruin you. I'll tell the university where that paper came from."

And there was the truth. The man she'd been so in love with? User. Master manipulator. Who had lured whom? Alex crossed the room and hung up the phone. He had her trapped. On the tenth floor of a building with no elevator and caught in his deceit.

Without Marc.

* * * *

Marc set aside his guitar. This was a waste of time. When Jason was in pain, he produced amazing music. All Marc could manage was to suck. No words, no music, no fucking anything. When he was with Alex, he had no trouble creating new music. The best he'd ever done. Jerry even liked the "Short Skirt" song and asked if he had anything else laying around he wasn't planning to use because he might be able to cobble a career for his one-hit wonder from Marc's cast offs. Jerry had said he thought Marc had grown as a songwriter and expanded his range, too.

Maybe he'd meant that patronizingly. Marc opened the e-mail. There it was. Grown as a songwriter. Expanded his range. Like he was some kind of goddamn kid who had to grow up. He needed a drink. Somebody would be up for a drink. Hopefully.

He climbed into his car, but instead of heading to Ty's house or to any bar on Sunset, he found himself on the highway to the office.

Marc pushed through the doors, expecting to see Jody perched at the reception desk, looking as pissed as she had since Jason got married. One would think that four years after he married Cassie, and had one child with another on the way, Jody would have gotten over losing Jason, but no. Then again, Jody wasn't at the desk either. He started down the hall. Sandy, the band's manager, had his door closed, but high-pitched women's voices came through the office manager's open door.

Helen sat at her desk with a baby in her arms. Candy, the band's publicist, knelt on the floor with a black-haired toddler, playing with blocks. Jody sat on the other side, reaching toward her with wonder in her eyes. That was a huge improvement over pissed. Bear's wife, Maureen, lounged at one end of the couch, leaning over with her elbows on her knees, smiling at the toddler. Tessa, the band's lawyer, perched at the other end, looking like she was afraid someone would try to hand her a child. Jason's wife, Cassie, straightened from where she had been leaning over the chair where her daughter Andi was sleeping. No wonder Sandy had his door closed. The whole Greek chorus was here. At least they would be good preparation for the harassment he was going to get from the band.

"Candy, you said one kid. That's two kids. Can't you count?" Marc said.

"Very funny." She tweaked the toddler's nose. "I couldn't leave June behind in China, could I? Just look at that face."

June grinned and went back to stacking blocks.

"Marc, you must see this darling baby!" Helen said. "Come here."

He obeyed because it was easier. The baby was like every other baby he'd had thrust in his face. Small and fragile. The cap of black hair reminded him of Alex, but what didn't? Eating had been nearly impossible since he came back from West Virginia because food in general made him think of her. Every tune he started playing turned into a dirge.

"You're home early," Cassie said. "What happened with Alex?"

"Your guess is as good as mine."

"Ida said she just up and ran off with no notice."

All of them were looking at him now. He'd been trying to brace for this for the past couple of days, but how did one prepare for the pity and disdain of every significant woman in one's life for not being able to keep a relationship together? If Connie and Suzi were here, he could get it all over at once. "All I can tell you is what I told them. Everything was fine between us when I dropped her off at her cousin's house. The next day when I went to pick her up after her shift, she was already on a bus back to school."

"Why was she still waiting tables?" Tessa asked. "Couldn't you afford to keep her in the style she was accustomed?"

Helen hissed at her.

"It's a valid question." Tessa folded her arms.

"She said Ida and Paul were counting on her, and she couldn't let them down."

"That whole family has always been very responsible, at least the branch in Potterville." Cassie settled on the floor, leaning on the desk. "They take promises seriously."

"And yet, she ran out on her job without giving notice," Maureen said.

"My point exactly," Tessa said. "So what did you do or say to screw it up, Marc?"

"Tessa!" Helen hissed and the baby started to cry. Marc wished he could join in. Might feel good.

Tessa kept her gaze glued on Marc. "The full report."

"It was great." He paused. So great she took off without a word. "I thought it was great. We got along. The sex was good. We could talk about stuff. We got into an argument that last day because a customer was manhandling her, and I told him to buzz off. Ida was going to kick him out because he had been there bothering her before."

"Who was he?"

"Beats the hell out of me."

"Watch your language," Candy snapped.

"The kid is what? Four? And she just got here from China so she doesn't speak English yet," Marc said.

"And I don't want her first words in English to be swear words."

"I want to be there when you tell that to Ronnie."

"Done, and he's okay with it. Now back to the way you have fudged up your life."

The chair was taken and no way was he sitting between Tessa and Maureen for this, so he perched on the edge of the desk. Helen had gotten the baby quieted down, so he didn't have that grating on him. He might make it through this interview with a little dignity. If he could buffalo reporters, he could fool the women in his life. Marc drew a deep breath and straightened his shoulders. Nah. "As far as I know, he was just some customer who'd developed a fixation on her. She got mad because she said she could handle it herself. I told her I loved her and wanted to protect her." It had been something along those lines. All he could remember was the expression on her face when he told her he loved her. That stunned amazement, like she couldn't quite believe it was true.

"You told her you loved her? You?" Tessa said.

"It was on Facebook," Maureen said.

"I must have missed that. Did you even tell Dez you loved her before you'd been married a year?"

"Someday somebody is going to explain to me why it is so fu—darn important to tell someone you love them. I show it all the time."

"You never have told me you loved me," Helen said.

"I never told my actual mother I loved her, and I send you flowers every Mother's Day and on your birthday."

"Still. It would be nice to hear the words."

Marc twisted so he was facing her. "Helen, I love you. You make my life livable. Happy now?"

"As a matter of fact, yes. Did this Alex tell you she loved you?"

"No."

"No? Not ever?" Jody asked. The other women shook their heads and frowned.

"Angela did tell me she was in some kind of weird relationship that just ended," Cassie said. "Maybe she was afraid to."

"What happened?" Maureen asked.

Cassie shrugged. "No one knows. Her family never met the guy. It was like some big, dark secret. Angela said she got the feeling the guy might have been her professor because of the way she talked about him up until the breakup. Angela said Alex always talked about him like he walked on water until this last year, and then she stopped talking about him at all."

Marc shook his head. "Couldn't be. Her advisor is married. She told me."

"And that means?" Helen said. "It's not like only rock star wives cheat."

"No, not Alex. She's—she—" She'd muffled herself when they had sex. She always seemed surprised when he wanted to do stuff with her in public. She'd almost been in tears at the house, asking him if he loved her.

Tessa stood up. "Cassie, I need your help with some research."

Marc half noticed them leave the office. He was too busy staring at a point on the wall. Alex? His Alex? She was so honest and forthright. How could she have been sleeping with her married advisor?

Tessa and Cassie walked back in. Tessa stuck a paper in his face. Roger Delgado, professor of literature. The notes scratched at the bottom of the page said he was married with two children, one five, the other a few months old.

"How do you get this information?" Marc asked to fill the silence while he absorbed what he was seeing.

"Give me half an hour and I can get his shoe size and what color loafer he prefers." Tessa settled on the couch. "I'm a lawyer moonlighting as a private investigator."

"No picture?"

Tessa glared at him. "There wasn't one on his staff page. Give me a few minutes."

"Is he the guy who was bothering her at the diner?" Candy asked.

"Maybe. I think so."

"So let's spin the scenario, shall we?" Candy stretched her arms over her head. "Ex-lover comes to town and begs her to come back. She's crazy about you, but you represent a real relationship and that scares her, whereas lover boy is the bird in the hand. So she runs back to him."

"Have you been taking fiction lessons from Suzi again?" Cassie asked. "Because this is the story I've seen play out over and over. Ex-lover comes to town after a nasty breakup that I'm figuring came around the birth of the new baby to the wife. Lover boy is trying to woo her back, and she decides the best way to make him hers is to go tell the misses, breaking up their marriage."

"Or," Tessa said. "Alex is blackmailing lover boy, and he went to WVA to tell her he wasn't paying any more, so she ran home to spill the beans."

"I can't believe that. Marc wouldn't be interested in someone that despicable. Didn't you say he was her advisor? What if he has something on her?" Helen asked.

"I don't care." Marc stood up. "She ran off and didn't answer when I called."

"Excuse me." Sandy stood just outside the door, clutching a piece of paper. "Maureen, do you happen to know where Bear is?"

"He said he was going to be working on the cars today." She turned to the other women. "It's that magical season of oil change."

They all snickered as if they didn't get all tied in knots over Christmas and birthday parties.

"He's not answering the phone," Sandy said.

"He probably can't hear it. When I left, he had the music cranked up in the garage. What's the emergency?"

"I just got a call from Rudy. Alan is having some kind of crisis and SendDown may need a fill-in drummer to finish out the tour." Sandy paused, giving all the women time to tense with concern, but not long enough for them to start demanding details. "Apparently, one of his drugged-out groupies just abandoned a child in a hospital somewhere, and he's decided he needs to become a model father. Tessa, I'm going to need you on this right now. I'm too old for this crap. This is why I never let you boys get mixed up with drugs. We had enough problems with the alcohol." Sandy glared at Marc for a second before stomping back down the hall. Tessa followed him out.

"But I never did anything!" Marc shouted after Sandy.

"You still smoke," Sandy shouted back.

Actually, he didn't. He hadn't even suffered the need to fiddle with a cigarette since Alex. Since she'd vanished from his life, he'd just felt empty.

"Speaking of which," Candy said. "How many times did you try to call her?"

"Alan has an illegitimate child abandoned in a hospital by a junkie groupie and I'm still the biggest elephant in the room?"

"Yes. As soon as Tessa gets the paternity tests back, I'll get my assistant on it. Until then, how many times did you call her?"

The dead could be rising and angels descending from heaven, and they would still want all the details of his latest breakup. They were worse than the Internet. He settled back on the corner of Helen's desk to finish the interrogation. "Once."

"Once? Did you send her a text or an e-mail?" Candy tapped her lips.

"I don't have her e-mail."

Maureen snorted. "You wouldn't."

"Why not?" Candy wailed.

"Because I didn't see a point. She took off without a word. I called. She didn't answer. If she wanted to call me back, I'm on her missed calls list, and she has the number."

"But you called her once. That doesn't shout 'I want you back.' Why not a text? If something terrible happened, she may need to know you want to hear from her," Cassie said. "She may have seen that missed call and thought you were checking what time she wanted you to pick her up. And when you didn't call again, she thought you moved on to the next groupie."

"Cassie, not everybody barricades themselves into the house when they get dumped." Marc smirked at her.

"First of all, I didn't barricade myself in the house, the snow plow did, and second, it was a pretty spectacular dumping."

"So was the reunion. You threatened to shoot him."

"I took him back."

"All very cute," Candy said standing up. "Are you going to explain why you didn't try to text?"

"I'm not going to end up as a social media joke." Marc folded his arms.

"Please," Maureen drawled. "Michael and I were on CNN. That woman Jason was dating before dumped him in *People* and you're afraid of Facebook? Coward."

"Look, I'm not going to chase after some little girl who freaked out because I mentioned marriage."

"You what?" Jody ran to the door. "Tessa come here. You have to hear this. Marc asked her to marry him."

"He what?" Tessa shouted down the hall. "Damn you, Marc. I already have one crisis on my hands, and I haven't vetted this woman. What is wrong with you?"

The baby started crying and Andi sat up blinking. "Mama?"

"It's okay, sweetie, Uncle Marc is just being a huge idiot." Cassie picked up her daughter and sat down in the chair with her. Candy took the baby away from Helen.

"I didn't ask her to marry me. I just mentioned a Joseph Campbell quote about relationships, and he used the word *marriage*."

"And you decided, instead of replacing marriage with a less inflammatory word, to stay true to the original quote," Helen said.

Tessa stepped through the doorway, rubbing the bridge of her nose. "The paternity test is done. It's Alan's. Jody, can you make arrangements for his parents to fly to San Antonio to pick the baby up? Helen, we need to contact that rehab facility for an immediate placement. Maureen, can you track down your husband and convince him to take over for the rest of the tour. Candy, your assistant has already sent me six e-mails and called three times that I know of. I think she's in over her head on this one. Sorry, ladies and Marc, but we have a code-red emergency on our hands. And, Marc, if you're going to propose to anybody else, would you try to give me a head's up first? Honest to God, you're turning into Tyler, and I can't take two of you."

"Here, Candy, let me help you get the kids to the car. Andi, honey, help me put the blocks away." Cassie scooped the blocks June had been playing with into their bucket while her daughter pushed the blocks that had gotten scattered toward her. "Marc, I never knew Alex very well because she only visited in summers, and she's quite a bit younger than I am, but she always seemed like a real nice girl. I'm sure whatever happened, she had good reasons to leave town the way she did."

"I think you really love this girl, Marc." Candy settled the baby in the crook of her arm and adjusted the strap of the diaper bag over her shoulder. "You're never this sloppy. I think you're going to have to take a page from the Jason Callisto Big Book of Stupid and jump in with both feet regardless of the consequences. Sometimes, that's the only way good stuff happens."

"Says the woman who went to China for one child and came home with two."

Helen's printer whirred to life behind him.

"Exactly. I wanted a family, and I went to China to get one." She patted his arm before taking June's hand and starting for the door with Cassie and Andi right behind her.

Marc turned to Helen. "And what are your words of wisdom, den mother dear?"

"No words. Plane ticket." She handed him a paper. "Go."

"I don't know. She's not calling me. What makes you think she wants me to show up on her doorstep?"

"Marc, darling, you came in here today to get permission to do just this." She stood and kissed his cheek. "Your flight leaves at seven forty-five tomorrow morning. I'm pretty sure Tessa has her address for you. Maybe you could try calling her to tell her you're coming. Go now. I have work to do."

"Before I go, why didn't you tell me sooner that Dez was cheating on me?"

Helen lost some color. "Oh, honey, I thought this was old news."

"I looked like an idiot for at least six months."

She leaned back in here chair. "I don't know why this is still bothering you."

"You knew, and you didn't tell me."

"You were touring, and it was such a tough tour. I didn't want to make things worse."

"Unnecessary roughness."

"You had a lot on your plate with that album doing so poorly, and the band being out of style. There didn't need to be any reason to cause unnecessary pain in the name of truth. I just assembled the evidence for when you were ready for it." She gave him a sad smile. "If you remember, I did drop a lot of hints, and I didn't tell anyone else here."

"Thanks, Helen. You handled it the right way." He held up the paper in his hand. "Wish me luck."

"Only the best."

He went down the hall to Tessa's office, but she was on the phone and deep in conversation when he stopped at her door. She held up a paper and rattled it at him. Handwritten in the middle was Alex Perkins, a PO box number, a building name, and the Chicago university. "Hang on." Tessa put her hand over the mouthpiece. "I couldn't get an exact address, but that's the building she lives in at least. You'll have to do a little of your own legwork on this one. No, I wasn't talking to you. Did it sound like I was talking to you?"

Marc walked out to his car. They were right. He had come here looking for permission, but he'd thought it was permission to let it go. But if he'd wanted to be told that he'd been right to let her go after she walked away from him, he should have gone to Tyler or Bear. They would have taken him drinking and told him how, if she wanted him, she would have stuck with him and not made him run after her. The women—they were designed to tell him to chase true love.

He scanned the papers. One-way plane ticket and part of an address. That would get him most of the way there, and then he'd have to camp out until she told him what happened. Even if it sucked, he needed to know the truth this time.

Chapter 9

"So everything is scheduled? No going back?" Alex asked, clutching the counter of the English office. Her stomach wanted to crawl up her throat, leap out her mouth, and run screaming into the street. Her heart agreed.

"All set. You look so excited." Annabelle, one of the English department secretaries, grinned at her, displaying crooked teeth along with her stunning lack of observational skills.

"Thrilled," Alex lied. Hey, she'd been doing it all day, why change tactics now? "Tuesday then. The Harper Room in the Student Center."

"Tuesday." Annabelle rattled her pen on the glass counter top. "I heard that Dr. Gregor has been telling everyone how insightful your thesis is. I had no idea you were even interested in Sylvia Plath."

"Yes, well, I guess when Melanie killed herself, it struck a chord with me." The lies felt like bathtub ring, waxy and vile.

Annabelle sniffed. "Poor Melanie. She really got caught up in *The Bell Jar* when we were in high school. Her father died when she was young, too."

"I didn't know that." Plath's or Melanie's? Great, now she needed to bone up on Sylvia Plath so she wouldn't get caught unaware at faculty mixers.

"I suppose it's not that surprising that you would develop an interest in Plath after studying Eliot. Plath had a deep interest in Yeats. I think she killed herself in Yeats old house, didn't she?"

What did Yeats have to do with Eliot? It's not like they were drinking buddies. "You know, I'm not sure."

"Dare I eat a peach, you know."

"Yes. Dare I." The thought of peaches made her want to puke. "You know, I'd love to stay and chat, but I have an appointment with my advisor." If the bastard was in his office. Then she could strangle him and go to jail instead of defending a dead girl's stolen thesis on a subject she knew nothing about to a committee who would endorse her if she'd typed the alphabet over and over again.

"Oh, sure. Last minute prepping. Good luck."

"Thanks!"

Alex tried to trot inconspicuously, but couldn't pull it off. A family touring the school turned to stare as she gave up and took the stairs two at a time. Roger's office door was closed. She hesitated outside. What did she expect to hear? Heavy breathing? Would Roger have the gall to cheat on the woman he was cheating on his wife with? Too bad the stolen thesis wasn't on Wodehouse. Her funny bone appeared to be at an all-time sensitivity. She knocked and waited. Roger was supposed to be working on a critical reading of *The Wasteland.* Because the world didn't have enough of those. Besides, he hadn't done most of the research. She had. He knew less about *The Wasteland* than she knew about Sylvia Plath.

Melanie had killed herself. She'd studied Plath so deeply that it killed her. Taking her thesis went beyond evil.

Dr. Gregor's office was one floor up. Dr. Gregor might have something to say about a thesis stolen from her dead graduate student on her area of concentration.

Alex ran for the stairs. From the hallway, she could hear soft jazz and the sound of muttering. Dr. Gregor stood on her desk in a pair of baggy jeans and a Cubs T-shirt, reaching for a book on a shelf that grazed the ceiling.

"Dr. Gregor?"

The professor shrieked and took a step back, planting her foot on her cup. Coffee splattered around the room as the mug went flying, and she tumbled behind her desk, knocking the chair into another shelf and bringing a pile of magazines sliding down on her.

"Oh, my God!" Alex ran around the desk. Dr. Gregor lay in a heap under the magazines with one foot hooked through the arm of the chair and her arms over her head. Alex reached for the magazine lying over her face. "Are you all right?"

"Alex Perkins," Dr. Gregor said. "Amazing what one misstep can do to you, isn't it?"

Had she hit her head on the way down? "Are you all right?" Alex repeated.

"My ego may never recover." Dr. Gregor glared at the bookshelf. "Didn't even manage to bring the book down with me. Shut the door will you?" She disentangled herself as Alex swung the door closed.

"I need to—" Alex started.

"I know." Dr. Gregor straightened her Cubs shirt and sat down in her chair. "I know what's going on. You're going to pass your thesis defense with no trouble, and from what I've heard, you'll be teaching freshman English by fall term."

"But it's not my thesis."

"Shhh!" Dr. Gregor looked around like someone might be hiding in her cramped office. "Welcome to the wonderful world of academia. You scratch my back, I'll scratch yours. Capiche?"

"What does he have on you?"

Dr. Gregor glared at her. "Never you mind. Just remember that I have something on you now."

"Please, what we have is mutually assured destruction."

"A wink is as good as a nod to a blind horse."

Alex straightened. "You've been watching too many spy movies."

"It doesn't matter. You're in it now, too. You out me for giving you Melanie's thesis and everyone knows you didn't write it. We're linked forever."

That would explain how Roger got his hands on Melanie's thesis. "But I didn't—"

"Doesn't matter." Dr. Gregor blushed. "All the university sees is a couple of cheating English professors, and what do you suppose they're going to do?"

"Fire us." For the first time in her life the thought of being fired didn't horrify her. It might even become a life goal.

"If it were only that easy. You and I, we're going to be trapped here for the rest of our lives doing whatever scut work no one wants. Just keep your mouth shut and neither of us spends the rest of our career going to inner city schools where you're more likely to get stabbed for your purse than recruit the next inspirational student."

Alex took a step back. Dr. Gregor, now Diana, as Alex would never be able to think of her as Dr. anything ever again, needed serious psychological help. "Well, I'll be going. See you Tuesday."

Diana narrowed her eyes and spoke in a super-villain voice. "Yes, you will."

Alex tried to grab for the door handle behind her, failed, and tried again. She knocked it open with her back and half fell out the door. The only other reliable place to look for Roger was his house. Carla might be there, but she'd have to take that risk.

She gave up all pretense of calm and ran to the bus stop. The two early arrivals already waiting took one look at her and stepped out of the shelter. Six years she'd been at this campus. Six. It had never looked so dangerous and shadowy before. On the bus, no surprise, she got a seat to herself. Through the windows, she watched the scenery slide by. She had never been to Roger's house before. He never invited her to mixers or had her bring anything from his office. Roger didn't want her around Carla, as Carla was such a harpy. She'd only met the woman twice.

See, that was the first mistake. Believing Roger's take on Carla when he went to such extreme lengths to keep them apart. Maybe she should have been watching more spy movies.

The bus left her two blocks down from the house. It was a beautiful neighborhood at the peak of summer lushness. Sprinklers swishing away, half a dozen little kids in bright bathing suits leaping through the water under the watchful eye of a slim older man with a copy of the Wall Street Journal under his arm, the dean of the psychology department trimming his hedges. How normal. The front windows of Roger's house were open and white curtains billowed through them. Bob Seger wailed about how rock and roll never forgot.

Hopefully, it did. Marc needed to forget all about her before he found out what she really was.

Before she could chicken out or Bob Seger started to sing another song that would remind her of Marc, she marched up to the front door and knocked.

The woman who opened the door had short strawberry blond hair in a kerchief. Carla. Where the hell was Roger?

"Alex!" Carla said. Her smile did not look out of place. Her face seemed to naturally fall into that expression. Hmm. "Hi. Come on in."

"Hello, Carla."

"I am so happy for you. Roger said you'd finished your thesis and were seeking treatment for your social anxiety this summer."

My what?

"Roger just ran out to get another gallon of paint. We're doing the dining room. You can join me for some iced tea while you wait."

Carla escorted her through the house to the kitchen. She was healthier than Alex expected, like she'd just walked out of a spinning class on her way to Zumba. "Jamie is at the neighbors and the baby is asleep upstairs. I feel like I haven't had five minutes adult conversation in a year. Roger tells me you switched your thesis to Plath. Poor Melanie. She used to babysit Jamie for us." Carla poured a tall glass of tea for Alex. "What drew you to Plath?"

Alex tried to open her mouth, but her lips were sealed shut. Roger described Carla as this depressed creature who was only interested in their child and spent her days watching soaps in a darkened house. Of course, Roger had also told Carla she had crippling social anxiety. Roger should start writing fiction. "I'm sorry. I shouldn't be here."

"Why?" Carla's gaze was wholly innocent and curious. "Am I overwhelming you? I'm sure it's not easy to deal with social anxiety."

"I don't have social anxiety. I'm not even shy."

"Really? But that was why Roger said you never came to our parties. You couldn't stand all the people."

Roger never wanted me to come to the parties because he knew if I got friendly with you, I'd dump him. As long as you were the shadowy monster Roger portrayed, I could somehow justify screwing your husband. And if I tell you now what's been going on for the past three years, it's going to break your heart, and now that I've met you, I like you and I couldn't stand to do that.

"I shouldn't be here." Alex stood up. She wanted nothing more than to flee back under her rock where all the slimy awful things lived.

"So soon? You haven't drunk your iced tea." Carla stood, too.

"I'm not thirsty. I'll talk to Roger tomorrow. Thanks."

Alex managed to walk to the bus stop more or less like a normal person. Her own life, she could ruin that. Diana and Roger, she'd enjoy taking down. Diana because she was nuts and Roger because he was evil. But Carla? How could she ruin Carla's life simply because both of them had made bad decisions about the same man?

Somehow she'd allowed herself to be maneuvered into this slaughterhouse chute and now there was no way out.

* * * *

Marc leaned on the counter of the little convenience store attached to the cafeteria beside Alex's building. The cafeteria was closed until the term started, but the convenience store was open, and the kid behind the counter was counting his lucky stars that he'd drawn the short straw and gotten this shift. "Here you go, man. Now, what can you tell me about Alex Perkins?" Marc slid the autographed photo across the counter.

"Wow. Total wow." The clerk burned a few seconds staring at the photo. "Alex Perkins. She's an RA in Montague." The clerk gestured in the direction of the building Marc had seen on the way in, but was now obscured by two walls.

"What's an RA?"

"She's in charge of her floor. Health and safety. Crap like that."

Well, that explained everything. Alex had a job being in charge of crap on her floor. This kid was a fount of vague and useless information. "Have you seen her lately?"

"I haven't, but Teddy, he's the other guy who works here, said she came back early from summer break and moved into her room. There's nobody much on campus right now. Summer session is over and freshman orientation doesn't start for another week."

Marc filed the information. Whatever it all meant, he might need it later. "Do you know where she might be now?"

The clerk shrugged. "Beats me. Unless she already has a book list and went to get her books. I think she's a grad student, and they can get pretty tight with the profs, so they can get their book lists early and avoid the jam up at the bookstore."

All fucking Greek, but more than he'd gotten out of the registrar. He was never going to get what he needed out of these people. He wasn't even sure he was asking the right questions. "But she's been seen here?"

"Teddy said he saw her. No reason for Teddy to lie. Why do you want to see her?"

The registrar girl had wanted to know that, too. Wouldn't give him any info, but thought he should tell her everything. "She's been doing some research for me."

"Oh, that makes sense."

The girl at the registrar had believed it, too. So college didn't require brains. Or maybe the brainy people managed to get out of working summers.

"She doesn't come in here much. She's pretty careful with her money, and she must get her groceries at the store." The clerk made it sound like she had a disease.

Marc leaned farther over the counter. "Now think. It's really important that I find her. Where could she be?"

"Um, I dunno." The clerk licked his teeth. "Wait. I'll call Teddy and see if he has any ideas." The clerk whipped out his iPhone and made the call. Marc feared for the future if this dipstick was it. After the initial explanation, the clerk's side of the conversation deteriorated to uh-huhs and okays. In the middle, he ran a bunch of register tape and Marc though he might have to revise his previous worry because Teddy seemed to have a bit more on the ball. Then the clerk said thanks and hung up. "Teddy says Alex is working on a master's degree in Brit Lit and she might be at either the library, her advisor's office, or his house." The clerk held out the piece of register tape that listed addresses for the three locations. Teddy did have it together.

"Great. Thanks a lot, man." Marc headed for the library first. If he saw Roger, he was going to belt him one, so he should put that visit off as long as possible. His phone started vibrating just as he started up the ramp to the library doors. Suzi. "Yeah?"

"Why are you looking for a Brit Lit tutor?"

"Why do you ask?"

"It's all over Twitter."

"Already?" Marc leaned on the metal railing. He couldn't have left the registrar's office more than an hour ago. The sun shone around him and several students walked past in a cluster, ignoring him and proving that he wasn't the center of the universe no matter what Twitter said.

"It started about half an hour ago, and the hashtag's really long already. You'll be pleased to know that your fans think you're smart."

"They think I'm smart?"

"Sure, several of them seem to believe you're some kind of literature scholar and that's why your lyrics are so complex." Her voice had been drifting a little so he assumed she was reading and not focused on him. There was a chance of getting out of this conversation without too much humiliation. His hopes were dashed when Suzi spoke again, clearly paying him full attention. "So why are you really there? Is it the girl?"

"Why can't it be because I'm a literature scholar?" He turned away from the path and leaned his hip on the railing. From this vantage point, he could watch bees going from one bright pink flower to the next.

"Because I know you. You don't have the patience to sit through the classes. You didn't have the patience to read *The Wasteland* when I gave it to you. You said it didn't make any damn sense."

"It doesn't make any damn sense."

"It does, but you have to spend a little time with it. So this is the girl from WVA? The deer?"

"Yes."

"Scared her off into the forest of academia, did you? What did you do, mention marriage?"

How did they all guess that right off? It wasn't like he proposed to every woman he dated. "You know, I hate it when you get all flowery."

Suzi gasped. "You did! You mentioned marriage! Do you like her that much? Scratch that, you're hunting her on her home turf, and Helen said you went to the office to talk about it. Marc, I'm so happy for you."

"Be happy all you want. I'm wandering around a college campus searching for her and failing. The kid at the store told me to try the library, her advisor's office, or her advisor's house."

"Why not her room?"

"I can't get her room number, just the building and a PO box number."

"Marc, there's not going to be a lot of people in that building this time of year. If you plant yourself at the door, she's going to have to walk past."

"And the entire world is going to see me sitting there like an abandoned pet."

"Aww, and you hate it when I get flowery. What building does she live in?"

"Montague."

Computer keys clicked on the other end. "I'm sending you the phone number of the resident director in that building."

"Alex is the resident director."

"Doubtful. A resident director job requires a master's degree in education. You said she's working on a master's in literature. The RD will be able to let you in the building. Turn on the charm. She's not supposed to let you in at all because you aren't a resident or maintenance person. You might have to tell her the truth."

"And what would that be?"

"Marc, don't be thick. You love her. Be honest. As long as the RD doesn't think you're stalking her, she'll give in to true love." Suzi took a drink of something. "Unless she's a nut."

"Thank you." Marc had meant to say it sarcastically, but it came out sincere. That sincerity traveled down his spine and the backs of his legs to the soles of his feet. "You're a good friend, you know that? Why didn't we ever hook up?"

"I have a boyfriend, remember?"

"Well, should this not work out and your thing comes unglued, I want you to keep me at the top of the list."

"Do you know something I don't know? Did I ask you about Gillian?"

"Gillian who?" She'd asked about this chick last time he talked to her. Damn it, whoever was road managing Savitar this tour had dropped the ball. Marc needed to remember to call the office and get this parasite kicked off the tour before she did damage.

"She's a groupie who's been riding with the band. And riding the band. You don't think Logan would…"

"Suzi, lay off the crazy juice. Logan knows there's a line of guys waiting to get their hands on you the second he screws up. He won't. Not if he knows what's good for him."

"Is that all that matters? That I'm the bone all the other dogs want?"

Was it? Marc surveyed the area in front of the library. Sunny, academic, bright flowers growing along the brick paths, students walking back and forth chatting. Suzi had been going to college when Logan met her, and now she was on the phone with him frightened and worried about Logan cheating on her, which he probably was. If he took Alex away from this, would she resent him? "Do you miss being in college?"

"Yes, but I wouldn't trade my life for anything." Something clattered on her end. Probably one of her endless cups of tea. "Marc, don't chicken out now."

"I'm not chickening out."

"Right now you are fishing for a reason to give up on this thing with the deer. You are standing in the middle of her university campus thinking you're going to ruin her life by being in love with her because you're listening to me be a basket case."

Whatever made him think he was attracted to smart women? "Suzi, you are not a basket case."

"Go get her. Even if this isn't forever, you can both be happy together for a little while."

She was right, but that didn't mean she had to have the last word. He could be a clever mind reader, too. "Go out to L.A. and hang out with your number one fan."

"My number one fan?"

"Brian."

"I don't think Logan would like that."

"Fuck Logan."

"He's not home. That's the problem, remember? Maybe I should go join him for a little while. That would keep Gillian away from him."

Marc took another look around. Suzi was far, far too smart to be saddled with that dip wad. "If that makes you happy."

"You going to find the deer makes me happy. Go."

"Fine. I hate you."

"Aww, I hate you too. *Buh*-bye."

Marc closed his phone. Go get her. Suzi made it sound so easy. Oh, yeah, the resident director. He opened his phone again to locate the number. Call her now or walk over to the building and call her from the door? She might not be in the building. This indecisiveness sucked. His feet didn't seem to want to commit to motion. Alex could have had a very good reason for leaving the way she did. The discussion about marriage could have sent her running. What girl that age wanted to be married to an old man like him? Unless she was a gold digger out for his money, which she did need but had never asked for. It would make her life better not to have college debt hanging over her head. The guy in the store said she was too careful with her money to shop there much and she'd been waiting tables in Potterville. She could probably use a cash infusion. Money wasn't a problem for him.

Instead of calling the resident director, Marc called Helen.

"Hello, lover boy. How goes the search for the perfect woman? I hear you're at her university."

Marc turned back toward the flowerbed. "You all need lives."

"Now, now, that's not nice, Marc. We're concerned."

"It's nothing to be concerned about."

"Are you still angry because I didn't tell you about Dez? I don't understand why this is coming up now."

"It's not about fucking Dez. I need you to do something." They all needed hobbies. He just wanted to do a nice thing for Alex, who dumped him.

"I don't think I want to talk to you right now."

"Well, you don't have a choice because you work for me."

"Wow, good-bye."

"Helen? Helen?"

Nothing. Damn it.

He found her number again.

"If you aren't planning to be civil, I'm not speaking to you. You boys do not get to act like trumped up divas in this office." Helen sounded like she wanted to take him over her knee. Wouldn't put it past her. He probably deserved it. Scratch that. He did deserve it.

"I'm sorry. I just don't understand this unhealthy fascination everyone has with my love life."

"What do you need?" Arctic. Positively arctic. Next phone call needed to be the florist for a nice big sorry-I'm-a-jackass bouquet.

"Would you please find out if Alex has any school loans and pay them off? And contact the university about paying her tuition for this year?"

"No."

"No?"

Nothing, but he could still hear her breathing.

"Helen?"

"I will not be party to another one of you boys trying to buy a woman."

"I'm not trying—Helen? Helen?" Marc looked at the phone. Dead. Unbelievable. He pulled up Tessa's number and called her.

"Too late. Helen already told me, and I have to tell you I am horrified," Tessa said when she picked up.

"I'm not trying to buy her. Why would you think I would be trying to buy her?"

"Because my brother tried to do it not too long ago. But if you're doing a good deed, let me put you on speaker so you can plead your case."

"No don't—" The phone chirped in his ear as she switched over. "Every one of you is into this public humiliation thing, aren't you?"

"Son, we only have your best interests at heart," Sandy said.

Wonderful. From the sound of things, everyone in the office today was clustered around Tessa's phone. Might as well get it over with. "I want to have Alex's debt cleared and next year's tuition paid so she doesn't have to worry about money so much. Is that acceptable?"

"Why?" Tessa asked.

"Because she worries about money, and I want to make her life better."

"Aww!" Jody squealed. "Tessa, you should do it."

"Shh!"

"Is that the only reason, Marc?" Sandy asked.

"Why would it not be the only reason? Why do I have to have an ulterior motive?"

"Because in general, you do?" Tessa asked.

"Shh! Marc?" Helen this time.

Yeah, everyone in the office to witness his humiliation. "Yes?"

"I'll take care of it. I'm sorry I doubted you."

"You'll what?" Sandy shouted. "Wait just a minute."

"No." Helen again.

The sound of the voices retreated down the hall. "Congratulations, Marc, you've caused a rift in the office."

"Thanks. That's what I was shooting for. And could you do one more thing for me? Call whoever is road managing Savitar this tour and tell him to get rid of Gillian."

"Ruby Case is with them and Gillian who?" Tessa asked.

"Beats me. Suzi keeps asking me about a Gillian."

"No problem. Good luck, Marc."

Marc hung up on the sound of raised voices. Sandy had been pulling out his dreaded teacher bellow to drown out Helen's mother scold while Jody had been trying to break in and was being ignored. He called the florist and arranged for flowers all around, and then added boxes of chocolate.

Before he could shove the phone in his pocket and get on with his little quest, it rang again. The ringtone he'd assigned to every member of SendDown. "Hello?"

"What the fuck are telling Suzi?" Logan. Damn it, just what he needed right now.

"At the moment, it's Suzi telling me." Marc fumbled through his pockets looking for a cigarette. Nothing. Damn it. He hadn't brought any with him because Alex didn't like them.

"She's in tears, screamin' at me on the fucking phone about how she wants to come tour with us. I don't want her around these assholes."

"Your bandmates?"

"My bandmates, those dicks in BroRide, the fucking roadies."

"So every man on the planet."

"You are such a dick. Wally is into her. He's on her the second she gets here."

"I thought Wally was her bodyguard."

"He is, but he's doing his job too good. I got to keep her safe."

"My ex-wife cheated on me while I was on tour because I left her at home." Marc started in the direction of Alex's building. She wouldn't be like Dez. Alex would be okay on her own with her nose buried in a book for weeks at a time while he toured. She probably wouldn't end up stir crazy and neurotic like Suzi either. Having Alex in the loop would be good for Suzi, too. Alex could present Suzi with intelligent arguments for dumping Logan's pathetic ass.

"Shit, you don't think some asshole in Rochester is moving in on her while I'm here, do you? I moved her there to protect her."

You moved her there to isolate her because you're an insecure sack of shit, but that's beside the point. "She's lonely in Rochester. I told her to go hang out with Brian."

"Brian. Why didn't I think of him? He'd protect her. Thanks, man, you're a genius."

"Yeah, thanks." Dip wad. Afraid of other men stealing his girlfriend, so instead of keeping her close and sexing her up, he sent her off to another rock star. Who was the genius here?

Marc stared at the dormitory Alex lived in. Yeah, who was the genius here?

He should go home. Just return to his life and give up on this thing with Alex. Yes, she was great, but was she worth all the *sturm und drang*?

She liked to play board games instead of relationship games. She read huge, heavy books about dead people and could talk about them like they were friends. She would watch baseball and ask questions. She was low key, calm and sarcastic. Even when she was pissed, she was quiet about it. Hanging out in Jason's living room with her, he'd been about as happy as he'd ever been without having a guitar in his hands. And she'd made that better! When he'd played Jason's latest brilliant brain fart for her, she'd compared the rhythm to some dead guy's poetry and found it on the Internet for him.

They were right. She was worth it. Even if it meant having to buy I'm-sorry jewelry gifts for everyone in the office.

He used the number Suzi sent him and listened to it ring three times before it picked up.

"Hello?"

"Hello, is this Cheryl Washowski?"

"It is."

"My name is Marc Wells and I'm—"

"I'm sorry, your name is what?"

"Marc Wells."

"Marc Wells from Touchstone?"

"Yes."

"Oh, my God, really? Why are you calling me?"

If you had let me finish, I would have told you. He needed a cigarette and a stiff drink. And Alex. "I'm looking for Alex Perkins."

"Alex, why? Are you really looking for an English lit tutor?"

Oh, goodie, a Twitterer. "Something like that. Can you tell me where she is?"

"I don't know. I suppose she's with her advisor, prepping for her thesis defense."

"She finished it? She told me she was planning on working on it this term and hoping to get it done by the end of the school year." Why would she lie about something like that? That was why she couldn't go to Italy. She'd have to take a semester off. Or had she not wanted to go to Italy with him? None of this made sense.

"She finished and handed it in not long before she got back. Got her defense committee all organized and everything. She defends Tuesday."

"But you think she's with her advisor now?" Marc fumbled the paper the clerk had given him out of his pocket. Address for the advisor's office and home. "Do you think she's more likely to be at his office or his house?"

"Why? Holy shit, are you here?"

"I'm right outside the building."

The phone clattered. Why the hell had he said that? He jammed the paper back in his pocket half a second before the front door banged open and a middle-aged woman launched herself at him. When she hit, he staggered back a step, but caught his balance before they tumbled into a flowerbed. Arms still wrapped around his neck, the woman stared at him. "It is you."

"It is me. Let go now, please."

She released him, turning crimson. "I'm sorry. I've just been a fan of yours forever. I can't believe you're here. Can I get your autograph?"

Sure, now that you've got my damn DNA all over you. "First things first. I'm looking for Alex. Do you think she'd be at her advisor's office or his house?"

"Oh, my God. You're the bad romance."

Bad romance?

"Alex looked destroyed that first day when she got back, and she said it was a bad romance." Cheryl clasped her hands together and pressed them to her lips. Her eyes were dilated, and her color had sunk to an unnatural pale. She was about to keel over.

"Do you need to sit down?"

Cheryl sat on the pavement exactly where she'd been standing, like his question had been an order. "It's always the quiet ones, isn't it?"

People were starting to stare. Why wouldn't they? This could not be a standard scene. "Why don't we step inside?" He hoisted her to her feet.

"I shouldn't. You aren't a resident, and the building isn't open, but I suppose you are a guest. You could be my guest. Marc Wells, my guest." She kept mumbling all the way to the building where she used her key to let them in. Straight ahead there was an elevator with its guts spilled out across the hall. She pulled left so he followed into a little lounge area with a television mounted high on the wall, a long cheap-looking table, and some square, very dirty aqua blue furniture. She dropped on a couch and cradled her face in her hands, now muttering about quiet ones and thesis and somebody named Gerald.

Marc paced the room. He should have bought a pack of cigarettes when he was quizzing the clerk in that store. They probably didn't allow smoking in here. Through the window, university life carried on. A group of groundskeepers arrived to attack an empty flowerbed. One of them clutched a Taco Bell cup in his scrawny hand. Some kids rode skateboards along the sidewalks. He could live here while he waited for her to finish out her degree. Not like the band would be doing anything until after Cassie had the baby. He could even get into some real literature and prove the Twitterverse right.

Somebody was walking toward the building, head down, very fast. Not quite running, but absolutely fleeing from something. He knew those delicate arms and the echo of them wrapped around him. He stepped toward to the window to study her. She didn't have anything in her arms. In one hand, she clutched some kind of little card carrier from which a key dangled, glinting in the sun. She was lovely. Even without seeing her face. Something in the way she moved exuded grace. For a moment, he lost sight of her when she got to the door so he bounded over hoping to catch her when she came through. When the door clanged open, Cheryl shot up from her seat, blocking his way out of the lounge.

"Oh, my God, it's Alex," she hissed.

"I know." Marc fought the temptation to grab the woman by her shoulders and hoist her out of this way. The outside door started wheezing closed and another door clanked. "Can you get out of the way?"

Cheryl opened her mouth again in the distinctive *O* shape that warned him another plea to the heavens was on its way, and he lost his fight. He clasped her shoulders as gently as he could manage under the circumstances and maneuvered around her.

The pneumatic hinge on the stairwell door was easing closed. He pushed through and heard Alex's footsteps running up.

"Alex!" Marc leaned into the gap between the railings. Based on the white fingers wrapped around the railing, she appeared to be on the third floor. "Alex, hold on."

Nothing. No footsteps coming down, no footsteps going up. Marc watched her fingers as he climbed. When he came around the fourth flight of stairs to the third floor landing, she was standing as if frozen with one foot two steps higher than the other and her hand with a death grip on the railing.

"Alex?"

She stood, staring down at him, poker faced. "What are you doing here?"

Marc put one foot on the bottom step. Somehow, the energy to climb up to her wasn't there, like she was putting out some kind of force field that wouldn't allow him any closer. "You left so suddenly. I was worried that something was wrong."

"Nothing's wrong. I submitted my thesis, and if I can get it approved in time, I might be able to have a teaching post here this fall. Everything's great." Her voice lacked all the music it had always had before. Now it was off key and toneless. If she'd been a guitar, he would have thought she needed work on her bridge.

"And yet you sound so happy." With effort, Marc hauled himself up a step. "Ida wasn't pleased."

"It was important that I get back here as soon as possible. Far more important than some waitressing job." She pursed her lips and then licked them. Nowhere near as sexy as usual. "I'm getting back together with my old boyfriend, too."

The deep dark baggage. "Oh?"

"When I came back to school, I saw him and we talked."

"And again, you sound so happy." Her entire body looked like it was carved from one piece of hard wood.

"It's none of your business."

Marc braced himself to attempt another step. This was like walking into a blizzard. He picked up two risers this time, bringing him to what should have been arm's reach and level with her shoulder. Up close, her face looked even more shuttered than it had before. He'd been mistaken about the hard wood. She was carved out of marble.

"I think it is."

"That's because you're a self-centered celebrity who thinks everything is about him. You—" She twitched and something awful surfaced under the marble.

"No, it's mostly because five days ago we were in WVA playing board games, watching *Airplane!* and talking about going to Italy, and twelve hours later you had vanished and everybody blamed me."

"I just woke up. There's no way you and I could have a successful relationship. I'm intellectually superior to you."

Marc blinked. It sounded like she'd just called him an idiot. Harsh. "Okay. You could have said good-bye, at least."

"I assumed you would have figured that out when I left town, but if it helps, good-bye."

She turned and walked up the steps. Marc stood listening to her footfalls all the way up, followed by the sound of the fire door at the top opening and closing.

Damn.

He stopped on the way out to leave an autograph for the resident director, but she'd already retreated into her apartment, and he didn't have the energy to deal with her so he signed her white board. Then he made his way back to the hotel feeling like the whole world was filled with cement.

She was just a girl, and too young at that. The world was full of girls. Girls and women. So what if he liked her and she was calm? She'd just kicked him to the curb. She'd also told him he was stupid. Twice. Just because he hadn't gone to college didn't mean he was stupid. What a bitch.

No, that wasn't right. The cadence of her speech, the way she held herself like she'd taken a mortal wound, the way she vanished. Something was very rotten on the state of Denmark.

Marc grabbed the phone off the desk. "Hi, I need a pack of index cards, a thing of yarn, and some tape delivered to my room."

Chapter 10

Alex opened Roger's office door without knocking. What was the worst that could happen? Catch him mounting a co-ed on the desk? That would be a relief. "I can't do this."

Roger jerked backward, his face turning gray like she might have taken a couple years off his life. He held his hands up in limp claws. His laptop was open on the desk so he might have been working on the book he'd been writing for the past three years. "Can't do what?"

"This thesis. I can't submit it as my own work when it's not."

"Alex, Alex. You're being silly again." Roger came around his desk, and she thought he was going to hug her, but then he reached around her to close the door.

"I'm not stupid."

"I didn't say you were stupid."

"You said I was being silly. That's a synonym for stupid." Alex put her fists on her hips.

"No, it isn't."

"The way you use it, it is."

Roger sighed, and it sounded just like he was telling her she was being silly again. "You must remember that you have done the work."

"This is Melanie Finch's thesis."

"But you did write your own."

"I didn't finish it, and this thesis isn't my work."

"All the work you have done to help me over the year would have easily been a master's thesis."

"All that work is published in your name."

"Precisely."

Precisely what? When had this gibberish he spouted made enough sense to her that she'd gone along with it?

Roger put his arm over her shoulders and guided her to lean against his desk. "Alex, we owe it to Melanie to do this."

"We owe it to Melanie to steal her thesis?"

"She was a sad, disturbed girl who did a lot of work to no good end. You have already done so much work, and you contributed so much to my book. It's like you already wrote an entire thesis and then some." He tugged her closer. "If you hadn't been so distracted with my book, you would have finished by the end of last year. This is going to give you back a year of your life."

Alex closed her gritty eyes. Did she want that year back at this price? "I'm not staying at the university once I have my master's."

"What do you mean? Of course you are. Darling, we have plans."

Why had she gone online looking for pictures of Marc last night? If she hadn't, she wouldn't have seen the pictures of herself with him looking so happy. It was Marc's fault. Tracking her down in the stairwell yesterday. She'd been trying to break it off—well, not clean, but leaving him out of the really corrupt parts. Better for him to go on thinking she was a crazy bitch than knowing what she really was.

"I told Carla this morning."

Alex's stomach lurched. "Told her what?"

"I told her I've been unhappy."

"Unhappy." Three years sleeping with another woman, and now he tells his wife he's unhappy? Did he consider this working on his marriage?

"She cried. I'm going to have to tread very carefully with her. I can't be responsible for her hurting herself or the children."

"I met her last week."

Roger stiffened. "When?"

"The day I got back into town. I went to your house looking for you, but you had gone to get paint. You were painting the dining room." Alex turned to him. The proximity was too tight. From this distance, she should be leaning in to kiss him. "She isn't anything like you described."

"She's been having a good summer. That visit with her family did her a lot of good."

What had she ever seen in him? Doughy, barely on the healthy side of pale, big fat liar. "You told her I had crippling social anxiety."

"I had to have a good reason for why you never came over. It would just be too difficult to have both of you in the same place."

"For who?"

Roger frowned like that should have been obvious. At least he hadn't used a nice word to tell her she was stupid this time. "For all of us. For you to be with your rival. For me to have the love of my life and my wife together. For Carla to realize when she saw us together. It wouldn't be fair to her."

To her. As much as Alex wanted to know what hold Roger had over Diana, she wanted even more to know what hold Carla had over Roger. Alex drew a deep breath and closed her eyes. That made everything so much worse. All the better to see Marc's face when she had told him she was intellectually superior. Yeah, superior. Marc would have been smart enough to get her out of this mess. He could have waltzed in here, formulated a plan, and executed it without anyone even feeling slighted because he was just so dang charming.

Roger kissed her cheek.

Alex flinched. "Roger, don't. I'm going to finish the year here. During that year, I'm going to apply to doctoral programs elsewhere." The University of California perhaps. According to the Internet, Marc was interested in studying literature.

"Darling, why? We're so close to having everything we've always wanted. I have a friend who rents a condo that is far enough away from campus that we won't run into any students. I'll be able to come to your place. It's waiting for you."

"I'm committed to the residence hall for this year."

"But you don't have to do that now. You'll have a real job."

"I keep my promises." Except for the one to Ida about working that breakfast shift, and the one to Marc about running away with him and being his one and only as long as he wanted her.

Roger scowled. His toy was not behaving the way it was supposed to. Poor baby. "I suppose this will allow you to start paying off your loans."

Loans. There were no more loans. Marc paid them off even after she'd told him to leave her alone. Told him he was stupid. Why would he do that?

And she was about to go through with the defense of a master's thesis stolen from a dead girl because Roger said it was expedient. Right from a certain perspective. What perspective could this possibly be right from?

"Roger, this is wrong. I'm going to the dean and withdrawing Melanie's thesis, and then I'm going to finish my own thesis, defend it, and find another university for my doctorate." *That I'm not even sure I want anymore. How many semester hours would it take to get a teaching license? Teaching high school English can't be that hard.*

"Darling—"

"Please stop calling me that." Alex pushed away from the desk and turned to face him. The office was so crammed with books that she couldn't get far, but it was enough for the moment that he wasn't touching her. Her chest hurt. Her eyes burned. Once, in a past life, she had been able to draw a deep breath, but that was a hazy memory now. She deserved a Darwin Award for throwing away a chance with a man who loved her to keep covering up this affair with a man who didn't even know what love was.

"You can't believe the dean will allow you to just withdraw your thesis." Roger shook his head. "You'll be kicked out of the program. Shamed and blacklisted."

Shit, she'd been wearing those rose-colored glasses again. The dean wasn't going to accept *Oops, this isn't mine* as a reason for withdrawing a master's thesis. Unless… "Not if I tell him you did it."

The noise Roger made hung somewhere between a derisive laugh and a cough. "Why would he believe such a story?"

"Because it's true?"

Roger smirked.

She should have known that was unrealistic. "Then you need to help me come up with a story that will keep us both in the clear. And your pal Diana Gregor." Alex pressed her fist into the desktop. "I'm going to the dean, with you or without you. At this point, I really don't care if I get kicked out of the program or who I take with me."

Instead of flying into a rage or panicking, Roger leaned back in his chair, shaking his head. "I don't understand. I thought you came back to me because you remembered how much you loved me."

"I came back because you threatened to destroy my career, and you submitted Melanie's thesis as mine. I didn't come back out of love. I came back out of fear."

Fear. The word caught on some Moby Dick-sized blackness in her soul, dragging it up so that it nearly occluded the fluorescent lights in the office. Alex reached back for support. Her hand landed on a thick paperback that felt too much like her Early British Writers book for comfort.

"Alex?" Roger stood, reaching for her.

"Don't." Alex put up her hand to stop him, but snatched it back before he could grab it. The last thing she wanted was for him to get that foothold again. It might start becoming reasonable to defend the stolen thesis, and from there, it was all downhill into the cesspool she'd been trying to climb out of for the past five months. A board creaked in the outer office. One of the other profs must be stopping in, or a student looking for a professor early. Either way, witnesses would keep Roger in check. "Roger, I meant what I said last spring break. I'm done. This is wrong. It's not fair to me. It's not fair to Carla. And it's not fair to Melanie."

"Melanie is gone. There's nothing you can do to hurt her now. I know you were good friends, but she chose to take her own life."

Alex clenched her fists. Was Roger insane or had he just started to believe the story he'd woven for her? "We were not good friends. We barely knew each other. Even if we were best buds and her dying wish was for me to use her thesis to get my degree, I wouldn't be able to do it. Can't you see that it's wrong?"

"Love is always right, and I do love you, Alex. You mean the world to me."

"If I mean the world to you, then why won't you let me go? I'll take all the blame for the thesis if you want. I'll take the blame for everything. Just let me go." Marc had talked to her. He had played board games with her and hung out. He had walked around town holding her hand, ushered her into his car, ate lunch with her. A woman at the diner had videotaped him saying he loved her. It was probably on YouTube by now. When she got back to the dorm, she'd search for it.

Marc had said he loved her and everyone in the diner had applauded.

"I thought you understood. I have to move very carefully with Carla. She's delicate."

Someone was muttering their way up the dim, narrow hall just outside Roger's office.

"I am not asking you to move in any direction with Carla, and she's delicate because she's depressed…except she's not, is she?"

"She's having a very good week. That was why I agreed to repaint the dining room. She was finally interested in something, and I wanted to support that. Before I can leave her to be with you, I need to know that she's stable."

Shock rolled up her spine and thundered out her mouth. "I don't what you to leave her, for me or not for me."

Roger opened his mouth no doubt to embroider another layer on his fiction, but froze as the office door swung open between them.

For one glacial moment, Marc just stared at them, his presence filling the doorway. Then his eyes blackened and his brows came together as his presence grew to darken the office, the building. "Surely, you are not serious."

"Don't call me Shirley," Alex quipped. The look Marc turned on her made her wish she was on a crashing airplane.

"Him? You dumped *me* for *him*?"

"Marc." Alex floundered as her desire to flinch away from him collided with her need to collapse into his arms, succeeding in slipping on a pile of books. She caught herself on a bookcase before she landed on her ass, and then wondered if she wouldn't be better off groveling at Marc's feet.

"Who do you think you are barging into my office like that?" Roger blustered. "Did no one ever teach you to knock?"

"The last time I saw you, I was kicking you out of a diner for manhandling her." His gaze swung back to Alex. "If I had only known."

"Marc, please—" He loved her.

"No." Marc dusted his hands together. "I'm out."

He couldn't have disappeared that fast, but the doorway was empty. "Marc!" Alex lunged for the door, but Roger grabbed her arm.

"Where are you going?"

"I swear to God, Roger, if you don't let me go I will go to the dean and tell him everything, starting with how you were sleeping with the undergrad who was writing your papers for you."

Roger went white and released her.

Alex ran out of the office and down the hall. Marc was pushing through the stairwell door. "Marc, wait."

He didn't stop. Alex's throat closed against a second plea. How had he even tracked her down in Roger's office? Why was he here at all? When she said good-bye at the dorm, he should have gone away before he found out about this. She shoved through the door. His footsteps were near the bottom. She started down the stairs double time. "Marc, please!"

He was waiting inside the door at the bottom of the stairs. "You left me for him."

"No, not really." Alex rubbed her forehead. Her breath hitched. Not now. No tears. If he had any respect for her at all, it would be gone with the first tear. "I never wanted you to know."

"What happened to Shakespeare?"

She blinked.

"No legacy so rich as honesty."

And she'd accused him of intellectual inferiority? She'd told him that quote once, days ago. "Marc, I'm sorry. Let me explain."

He folded his arms.

Alex sat down on the steps before her legs gave out. The truth. She owed him that. Then he could walk away hating her for the right reasons. "I... Roger and I—"

"You're having an affair with your married professor."

If he knew, why was he making her tell? "Was. Was having. Past tense. I have been trying to get away from him for years, but he kept convincing me to stay. Until last March. I told him it was over at spring break."

"So what are you doing here?" His arms flexed in his black T-shirt.

"It's complicated."

"Use small words that an idiot like me will understand."

She was as bad as Roger. "I'm sorry about that. I never should have insulted you that way."

"No, you shouldn't have." He unfolded his arms and sat down beside her. "Alex, I don't know what I'm supposed to do here."

Alex rubbed her face and turned her eyes to the ceiling before threatening tears could escape. A good-sized cat was climbing around on her lungs after using her stomach as a litter box. "Can we go somewhere private so I can explain?"

Marc picked his cuticles in silence for some short eternity, but the rectangle of sunlight on the floor in front of the door didn't move so it couldn't have been more than a minute. "I still love you, Alex. I was pretty pissed off this morning when I worked it all out, but even I'm bright enough to know I wouldn't have spent the night in a hotel room tacking index cards to the wall trying to figure this out if I didn't love you."

Alex sobbed and curled over her knees.

He started rubbing soothing circles on her back. "I'm going to assume from this that the feeling is mutual."

She nodded without lifting her head. Her face felt scalded. "I just never wanted you to know. I know how you feel about people who cheat on their spouses, and I knew if you found out I was the instigator who led a man away from his wife, that you would hate me."

His hand on her back stilled. "You what?"

"I didn't mean for it to happen that way. I just looked up to him, and I wanted him to like me. He was so smart, and I thought he was handsome. I just thought—I don't know what I thought. I didn't think I was making him fall in love with me." Alex swallowed, trying to loosen her throat so her voice wouldn't sound like air escaping a balloon. "I'm sorry. We shouldn't be doing this here. Someone might see."

"I don't care if you don't." He resumed his slow circles.

"But if someone sees us they might—"

"Tell my wife? I'm short one of those right now. You must be confusing me with your last boyfriend." Marc stood. "Alex, stand up."

She wrapped her arms tighter around her knees, praying for a hole to open up and swallow the entire building.

"Alex." He crouched in front of her. "Darling, we can't do anything here. You wanted to talk in private so let's go someplace private to talk. Alex."

She tried to suck in a breath through her nose, but the way she was crunched up, she failed. Then Marc had her by the shoulders and was pulling her up. She wrapped her arms around him as he cradled her to his chest.

"Your dorm is close. Let's go there." He stroked her hair.

"I have to talk to the dean and get him to let me withdraw that thesis. I'll tell him it was my fault. That'll end this faster and with less of a cloud over the department."

"What thesis?"

"Roger submitted a thesis I didn't write under my name. I have to figure out how to withdraw it without getting anyone but me in trouble."

"Why are you taking the blame for something Roger did?"

"Penance."

Marc pressed his lips into a thin line and drew a deep breath before speaking again. "Is that what you want to do?"

"I have to."

"You should stop at the bathroom and wash your face first."

"Do I have to?"

"Yes, I think in this case I might be experientially superior to you."

"Are you going to keep bringing that up?"

"Hopefully for the rest of our lives."

* * * *

Alex left him outside the bathroom while she washed and prepared herself for meeting the dean. Her knees felt like she'd just walked away unscathed from a forty-car pileup, but her stomach wasn't so sure she hadn't caused it and still expected to be jailed for manslaughter. Somehow, she had to make the dean understand that she couldn't defend Melanie's thesis without letting him know it was Melanie's thesis. Unless she walked in and told him the truth. That had gone over so well with Diana after all. No, best to withdraw the thesis without the cloud of outright theft and faculty impropriety.

From the hall, she could hear voices. The hair on the back of her neck turned to needles. Marc's confident baritone countering Roger's less confident tone. She threw herself out the door, landing right between them. Marc leaned on the wall to the left of the door with his arms folded, his mouth pulled into a sneer like he was looking at a wet garbage bag that had just broken on his clean kitchen floor. Roger, standing in the middle of the hall, was more rumpled and pudgy than usual, like a deflating balloon. His eyes were red as though he'd been crying.

"Marc. Roger." Alex looked from one to the other, trying to rewind and clean up the audio of her memory so she could figure out what had been said before she came out, but her brain was not Memorex, and she lacked the advanced gadgetry they used in all of Finn's police procedural shows. She would need to invest in an upgrade soon.

Roger pointed one stubby finger at her. "You will not get away with this."

Alex blinked. She'd been under the assumption that she was in the middle of damage control. She had no clue what Roger thought and at the moment didn't have the faculties to figure it out.

"Pardon?" Marc had plenty of wits to work with. He was still smirking. And she'd told him he was stupid.

"I will not allow it."

"Sorry, buddy, but I think it's been taken out of your hands." Marc straightened. "You know how they say when God closes a door He opens a window? I'm Alex's window, and I'm pretty sure I'm a skylight."

Roger stared at Marc.

Marc turned to Alex. "Too flowery? I was talking to Suzi last night."

Alex held up a finger. "Let's address that in a minute. Roger, I'm withdrawing the thesis. That's all."

Roger ignored her. "If you go near my wife, I will ruin you."

"What are you going to do? Get me kicked out of school? Your wife has a right to know, and trust me, if I *just* ruin you after this, you'll be lucky." Marc's smirk had turned felonious. "I have friends with very long reaches and vindictive streaks. You have no idea."

"Stop. Just stop," Alex said.

Roger went pale. This time when he poked his finger at them it was shaking. "You stay away from me and my family. I'll tell the police you threatened me." Roger walked a few steps down the hall. Stopped. Turned back. "I'll get a gun." Then he ran out of the building.

"What's he going to do? Shoot Tessa through the phone?"

"Who's Tessa?"

"My lawyer. I'm not sure what we're suing him for yet, but we'll come up with something." He put his arm around her shoulders. "Let's go take care of this thesis thing."

"Do we have to tell Carla?"

"We do. Trust me, this is important."

Suddenly, talking to the dean wasn't so threatening. Alex led him to the bend in the L-shaped hall. The English department door was open, and a student secretary with a nose ring stood behind the counter sorting reading lists. "Can I help you?" She didn't even look up.

"I need to see Dean Meyer for a minute. It's urgent." Audible at least. Intelligible even. Alex peered down the short, shadowy hall that led to the dean's office.

"You're kidding."

"No."

The girl shook the papers at her. "Do you realize these frigging things have to be hung up to-fracking-day and they are in no order at all, and that rat bastard Jeremy called off with laryngitis, and Annabelle is just too good to work this week because this is the week all the grunt work has to be done."

Marc leaned on the counter, turning up the wattage on his charm. "I'm not going to be doing anything while she's in her meeting. Maybe I can help while I wait."

The girl's pout deepened. "We have to rip down all the old ones, but the stupid staple puller thinger is missing."

"I can improvise. I'm good with my hands." He spread one hand on the counter top and Alex experienced her first hot flash even though menopause had to be decades off yet. She could attest to how good he was with his hands as well as other parts of his body.

"Shit." The girl put the papers down. "He's in his office. I'll see if he can see you."

Alex placed her hands on his chest. She'd run away from this? How important were career and reputation when she had a hot man willing to stoop to fixing dishwashers and doing clerical work for her? "You aren't planning on improvising with those good hands on her, are you?"

"I'll save the special improvisation for you, but if I can get you the meeting you need by pulling a few staples, it's worth it." He kissed her, lingering for just a moment before leaning back to stare into her eyes. "Surely, you don't think anyone could tear me away from you."

"Don't call me Shirley."

He kissed her forehead.

She took a deep breath, drawing strength from him. All of this was manageable. Get the thesis thing dealt with. Talk to Carla. Finish her own damn thesis. Go to Italy. Live happily ever after. "I love you."

"I know." He gave her a lopsided smile that made her heart lurch.

The secretary clomped down the hall. "Okay, he said he can give you a couple of minutes if it's urgent, but he has a lot of shit to do today, too, so you can't be in there long."

Alex couldn't fathom the word "shit" coming out of the Dean's mouth, but the intent was clear. "I'll be quick."

As she left the outer office, Marc was leaning over the counter asking what the secretary needed help with first. The dean's door was down a short unlit hallway. He sat behind his desk, studying the computer screen. A frown was set into his schnauzer-like features.

"Dr. Meyer?"

"Ah, Miss Perkins!" He stood, waving her toward the chairs in front of his desk. "How lovely to see you. Did you ever manage to find that book?"

Book? She'd had him for Major American Literature. They'd studied only Jewish writers. One of the books centered around the daughter of an obscure writer only remembered for a short story, *Street of Crocodiles.* "No, I didn't, but I did find a film that referenced it. It was in a film festival of Post-Soviet Eastern European animation."

"Brilliant. Is it on the YouTube? I would very much like to see it."

"I'll try to find it for you and send you the link."

"Yes, good. Then Genesis can show me how to play it. Genesis is a lovely girl. You know her from the desk?"

Genesis, the overworked scowler. "We've met."

"Very good. Now, what was it you needed to talk to me about?"

"It's my master's thesis."

"Oh, yes! Congratulations. I knew even when you were an undergrad, someday you would be here on the faculty with us. I look forward to attending those boring parties with you. You will be a bright spot in the room. Dr. Wittier was saying to me just the other day, he also looks forward to it, but he didn't understand why you would want him on your defense committee."

Alex blinked at a sudden rush of tears. Looking forward to her being on staff? A bright spot in the room?

"My dear girl, what is it?" Dr. Meyer came around his desk and sat in the chair across from her, enveloping her hands in his. "Surely, you are not nervous or afraid to fail."

At least the joke didn't spring off her lips unbidden this time. He had that papery skin old people get, and his hands were dry on hers. Dr. Meyer had been the dean of the English department since she'd started here and she had to disappoint him. This was going to be a lot harder than she had anticipated, and this wasn't the worst she had yet to face.

"I'm afraid…" Her voice graveled to a stop. If she couldn't disappoint him, how in hell was she going to tell Carla she'd been sleeping with her husband for the last three years?

"But you will do well, my dear. You were always an insightful student, and a defense in this case is a formality."

Crap. He thought she was just scared to do the defense. He wasn't going to let her out of it unless she had a valid reason. Plagiarism was plenty valid, but the truth about this thesis was so incredible Alex wasn't sure she believed it herself. She'd never even read the thesis submitted under her name. But if she spun the truth just right, taking all the blame on herself for the theft, it had to believable enough for him to cancel the defense. "I'm afraid I…plagiarized it."

Dr. Meyer stiffened and drew a sharp breath. "Plagiarized? Are you sure? You are the only student studying Eliot at this university. Romantic poetry is not as in fashion as it once was. Your advisor is Dr. Delgado, yes? He is our resident Romantic expert."

Resident Romantic expert? Right, from a certain point of view.

"How could you plagiarize from another student? You?"

This was conditioning for when she told Carla. If she could live through this, she might be strong enough to survive that. "You haven't seen the thesis, have you? I changed my topic. Last Christmas when Melanie Finch killed herself, I was upset, and I changed my topic to Plath in honor of her. We were very close." Alex needed to find out where Melanie was buried so she could leave flowers on the grave for all her lies.

"I didn't know. You could have gone to the University Psychological Services for counseling instead of doing something so drastic as to change your thesis topic. Did your advisor approve it? I must speak to him about this."

"He did, but it's really not necessary to talk to Roger—Dr. Delgado, I made a very persuasive case." Alex closed her eyes, trying to block out the memories of her "persuasive case." "I had some of Melanie's notes, and I'm not sure now which conclusions are hers and which are mine."

"Alex, Alex. I am disappointed." Dr. Meyer withdrew his hands from hers and steepled them in his lap. "You must tell me who else knows about this."

Marc, Diana Gregor, Roger who started it all. "No one."

"Well, we will keep it between us, shall we?"

He couldn't be about to suggest she go ahead and defend Melanie's thesis as if it were her own.

"The university, it cuts the English department budget every year. If this were to get out, they would have reason to cut further."

He was. The world was mad. "Dr. Meyer, I can't present this work as my own."

"No, no, of course not." He patted her arm. "We can't reward plagiarism. We just need to keep this mistake of yours between us. But you came to me, yes? Before the real crime is committed. You and I, we will keep this between us. We will cancel the defense and you will complete the work you had started on Eliot."

A loud, excited squawk from reception startled them.

"Genesis. She is a lovely girl. Alex, is this acceptable? You will not speak to anyone?"

"No, I won't tell anyone." Not for all the tea in China.

He patted her arm again. "You have always shown such good sense that I cannot condone the destruction of your scholarly reputation for a misstep such as this."

If he only knew. Tears threatened. He was such a nice man. "Thank you, Dr. Meyer."

"Of course. Of course." He stood so she followed suit. "I still look forward to seeing you on the faculty. Just not as soon as we hoped."

"Thanks again, Dr. Meyer." If she had never bought that first cup of coffee for Roger, if she hadn't been that sweet little sixteen—nineteen— she could have been on his faculty. As she left, Dr. Meyer was settling down to squint at his computer again, and her heart sank as she closed the door on a life she'd never get.

Genesis sat on the floor in the reception area, bouncing as she talked on the reception phone. "... and she was so cool!"

Alex found Marc in the hall, prying old reading lists off the bulletin board with a pen. "What's going on with Genesis?"

"I thought Phil Collins wasn't interested in a reunion."

"What?"

Marc turned to her with the Great Books list dangling from a staple. "What?"

Alex pointed over her shoulder into the office. "What's going on with her?"

"Oh, she found out that I know Suzi so I called her up so she could talk to her. Now she's calling everyone she's ever met to tell them."

"Called who?"

"Suzi."

Alex shook her head. "This is turning into an Abbot and Costello routine."

"Who's on first?" He dropped the paper in the gunmetal gray trashcan beside the door. "How did it go?"

"It's done."

"One down."

"Let's save the other for later. It's been a long day already."

He pried off the last paper and dropped it in the trash. "Your place or mine?"

"Mine is closer."

Marc leaned into the office, put the pen on the counter, and waved at Genesis who was still burbling on the phone about the very cool Suzi, whoever she was. In the hall, he draped his arm over her shoulders, not caring who saw them. "What was the upshot?"

"Let's get to my dorm first. It's all very hush-hush."

"Cool."

Alex leaned her head against his chest. "We're going to have to talk, too, aren't we?"

"Yeah."

"I may cry."

"I'm adapting." He led her along the sidewalk like he'd lived on campus for months, taking her to the front door and waiting while she opened it.

Cheryl wasn't lurking in the lounge like she had been when Alex left. They hurried through to the stairwell.

"The elevators should be fixed by Wednesday. I'm going to be kind of sad when they are. It's been nice these last few days to go up to my floor and know that nobody else would brave all these stairs to get to me." She rounded the landing on the third floor and started up toward the fourth. "That's probably a little creepy in retrospect. Melanie lived on the tenth floor of the Liwa building, and that's how she killed herself. She jumped out the window in the middle of the night over Christmas break. Groundskeepers found her the next morning when they were shoveling the walks."

"Alex, slow down."

She turned back. Marc stood on the landing below her.

"Darlin', I smoked for a long time, and I haven't quite managed to quit yet."

She bounded down the stairs. He was short of breath.

"Okay."

"You're happy." He pulled her close.

"I'm so glad to have that thesis thing out of the way. Ever since Roger showed it to me, it's been hanging over my head."

"What did you mean you were the instigator with Roger?"

All that happiness? Poof. Her stomach dropped and her hands went cold. "I didn't do it on purpose."

"Tell me how."

Alex pulled away. "I brought him coffee." She sat down on the steps. "He was just so impressive. At least he was then."

"Did you drug the coffee?"

"No."

"Show up at his office in lingerie or something?"

"No, I just brought him coffee to class a few times."

Marc sat down. "I don't want you to take this the wrong way, but there is no way a woman brings me coffee, and I fall so madly in love with her that I cheat on my wife."

"I brought you a steak."

"I wasn't married."

"I guess." Alex tried to stand, but he caught her and pulled her into his lap. "I did this. I pursued Roger, and I knew he was married. Don't tell me I didn't."

"But you didn't." He turned her chin with his long fingers, forcing her to meet his eyes. "Alex, a cup of coffee doesn't make you a siren."

"It wasn't one cup."

"If you were a barista in a Starbucks, you wouldn't have wooed a man away from his wife on coffee alone. Men who want to cheat on their wives will find someone. Men who want to be faithful can resist anything, even if it's painful. Trust me. Sometimes it's agonizing."

"Don't get shitty and sarcastic with me. It was more than the coffee and you know it." She pulled away and walked up a flight of stairs. "I studied him to figure out what he liked. I paid particular attention to the works he commented on in class and focused on those. I watched to see which girls he watched in the halls and dressed like them. I changed my major from journalism to English because it meant more chances to talk to him and take his classes."

Marc walked up to join her on the landing. "So?"

"I did the same thing to you." She walked up another flight of stairs. He wanted truth? He was getting truth. "Let me tell you, the Internet makes that shit a lot easier."

Before she could escape up another flight, he caught up to her. "As far as I can tell, most people do that, and it is easier with the Internet. I have fans who are never likely to meet me in the flesh who study me. There's a woman in Iowa who has an entire blog devoted to studying my dialect."

She pulled away.

"Alex."

"You sound pretty Standard American to me."

"She went bananas when I said in an interview that the album we were working on 'needs mixing.'"

She took two steps at a time. In her room it would be safe to break down.

"Alex."

She stopped in the middle of the steps.

"Why do you keep running away from me?"

"I'm not. I'm walking up the stairs."

"Ahead of me. Every time I catch up, you take off."

Alex looked up and down the steps. He was still on the fifth floor landing and she was half a flight ahead of him. "I'm not running away. I'm trying to get up to my room. We're only halfway." Running away. Totally running away. Should have gone into psychology.

He climbed up beside her. "What did you do to attract me?"

"I analyzed your ice cream flavor choice."

"And what did you learn?"

"Butter pecan means you are conscientious, careful with your money, and you are a strong believer in right and wrong." She watched his face, but his expression didn't change. No way to tell if he thought she was nuts or not. "And I wore high heels and a short skirt to the diner that one day because I knew you were coming in."

"Most girls wear high heels and short skirts to meet me. The ice cream analysis fits though."

Alex pulled back. "You're being sarcastic again." She stomped up to the landing.

"I'm not. Quit being so fucking sensitive."

"I'm not being sensitive."

"Like hell."

Alex stopped next to the graphic six next to the door. She was being sensitive. And now she wanted to cry again. "It doesn't bother you that I tried to remake myself to be your perfect woman which was the same thing I did to Roger?"

"Not really. My buddy Bear lied to his wife when he first met her, and led her to believe he was a mechanic because he thought she would run screaming if she found out he was a drummer. That idiot Jason bought that land his house is built on to make Cassie love him. Dez, Jesus, I don't even want to go into the lies Dez worked on me."

"You divorced Dez."

"Exactly. No, wait. That's not where I was going with this." Marc started up ahead of her. "What I'm trying to say is that everybody I've ever known, when they wanted someone to like them, they bent the truth a little until they got comfortable with each other."

"You realize that makes no sense. Lie until you can tell the truth? What kind of a basis for a relationship is that?"

He stopped on the seventh floor. "Okay, not lie then, but be willing to test new self images to attract a desired partner."

"Gee, that doesn't sound clinical." Alex passed him, but he caught her hand before she got off the first tread and turned her toward him.

"Maybe it does, but I'm still not sure what the hell you were talking about when you were telling me about that Shelley guy."

"And you pretended to be following right along."

"I didn't want you to think I was an idiot." His gaze locked onto the cinder block wall behind her head.

Alex cupped his cheek. "An idiot? No. Too clever by half and three-eighths."

He wrapped his arms around her waist and kissed her, opening her mouth with his. Alex leaned in, grateful to have him supporting her. He slid his hand up her spine, bending her toward him and taking more of her weight.

"Alex," he said. His voice was strained and needy.

"We have three floors to go."

He groaned and released her, only to catch her hand.

"You said your friend was an idiot for buying that house to make Cassie love him, but you paid off my loans and paid this year's tuition."

"First of all, there was no house there when he bought it, and second, he bought the land to use against her. I paid off your loans just because I wanted to do something for you. Trust me, I got in hot water with the office and caused a major division between Helen and Sandy because they thought I was doing a Jason. I think they've got it sorted out now, though."

She had stopped when he said he wanted to do something for her, but he didn't notice until he got halfway up the flight. Their linked hands stretched their arms between them like a string of Christmas lights.

"What? I talked to Candy last night, and she said she talked to Sandy yesterday and everything is smoothed over now."

"You just wanted to do something for me? But I told you I didn't want to see you anymore, and that I'd gotten back together with my boyfriend. I told you it wouldn't work out because you were intellectually inferior."

He came back to her this time, still cradling her hand. "I thought we weren't talking about that anymore."

"It seemed pertinent."

"In the interest of full disclosure, I told Tessa to clear your debt before I found you at your dorm, but I could have called her back to cancel, and I didn't. You were worried about money."

"When did I say I was worried about money?"

"You said if you took a semester off, your loans would come due. Besides, what college student isn't stressed about money? I could fix that for you."

"Even if we weren't sleeping together?"

His jaw flexed and he blinked a couple of times. "I guess. I want you to be happy even if it's not with me." He squeezed her hand. "As long as the guy is somebody better than me. If you could find that mythical beast. A man better than me? Doesn't exist."

She laughed, but the sound that came out was more of a strangled sob. He wanted her to be happy. He wanted her with a better man if she wasn't with him.

"You gonna cry?"

"I thought you'd adapted."

He put his arm around her shoulders. "Work in progress." He led her up the stairs.

"You've never lied to me."

"Except for pretending to have an interest in poetry, no. I did end up being interested in it, though, so I guess I did try on a new self image and I liked it." His phone rang. With his free hand he fished it out. "Hello? Can't talk. No, not eating, smartass. I'll check in later." He stashed the phone back in his pocket.

"Who was that?"

"Bear. He's never going to let me live this down."

"Live what down?"

"Love at first sight."

"Love at first sight?"

"You." He stopped on the ninth floor landing and stepped back far enough to see her face. "I've never done this before."

Alex shivered. The moment demanded she ask what, as if she didn't already know, but there was no purpose in it. It was her. It was falling in love in a week. It was throwing himself into the moment with everything he had. Her whole body trembled, wrung out and dehydrated.

"Don't worry. I'm sure Jason is working on a fucking brilliant power ballad about it right now. He'll be done in an hour, and it'll go platinum." He shrugged.

Alex pushed him back against the wall. "Let him write the song. We get to live it." She pushed her hands under his shirt, stroking the firm muscles of his abdomen. Stretching up on her toes, she kissed him, needing the contact. He hooked his hands around her thighs, pulling her up his body and dragging his hard length down her belly to right where she wanted to surround him. She wrapped her legs around his waist as he rolled her against the wall. She twined her fingers through his hair, catching his earlobe between her teeth.

"We have one more floor to go," he murmured against her throat.

"I don't care."

"I care about you." He shifted and started carrying her up the stairs. "No more sex on desks in offices. No more shitty hotel rooms. No more closets. No more hiding. No more quickies."

She bit his neck. "No more quickies?"

He set her down at the tenth floor door, breathing hard. "Okay, we can have quickies, but not every time." He pulled the door open. "Get out your keys before you make me break my promise already."

Keys. Oh, yeah. Several years ago when she left this morning, she'd crammed them in her pocket. They were still there on the ring with her student ID. She opened the door and walked down the short hall. Marc met her in the middle of the room after he closed the door, not giving her a chance to speak before her slid his hands along her jaw and into her hair, drawing her face to his. She splayed her fingers on his back, pressing as close as she could. He was hard in all the right ways, and yet so gentle, cradling her against him. One of his hands left her for a second.

"You are so lucky I'm a boy scout." He shifted back a step, holding a foil covered condom between his first and second fingers. "I went over there expecting to yell and be yelled at for a couple of minutes and came prepared anyway."

"Am I supposed to call you a good boy?" Alex reached back and pulled open her desk drawer where her box of condoms lived.

"Clever girl."

"You knew that." She pulled her T-shirt over her head and unhooked her bra.

He pulled off his own shirt before drawing her against him again. Instead of taking her down into another breath-stealing kiss, he simply stared at her, grazing his fingers down the side of her face. "You're so beautiful. I was afraid I'd lost you."

She had no words. The way he looked at her filled her with wonderful emotion, but she couldn't compose a single sentence to tell him that.

Whatever he learned looking at her face seemed to be the response he needed because he picked her up and carried her to her narrow bed, laying her down before kneeling beside her. He kissed down the center of her torso, working open her jeans. Standing, he pulled the jeans off her. Then he removed his own, slipped on a condom, and stretched out beside her. Skin on skin, Alex twisted toward him and hooked her leg over his hip. Holding her gaze with his own, he slid inside her. She clenched her teeth as the sweetness of it overtook her.

"It's okay." Marc whispered, setting a slow, easy rhythm. "You don't have to hold back."

"Hold back?"

He thrust hard, forcing a moan out of her. "Just like that. We don't have to be quiet." He braced his hand in the small of her back, increasing his rhythm.

Her breath came in short gasps as she buried her face in the curve of his neck. One arm was wrapped under his body, and she clutched her fingers trying to find purchase on his skin. He shifted up on his elbow with his hand under her head, looking down at her like she was priceless. The slight change hit a new spot when he thrust, sending another crackle of electricity through her. She bit back a startled cry. He pulled her leg higher. She threw her head back struggling to stifle herself, but this time his every motion was exquisite. The feel of his heavy breaths across her shoulder made her aware of his harsh grunts. Someone would hear him. Someone would know.

When she looked at him, he was staring at her. Drinking in the sight of her. A breathy gasp escaped her. Then another. Then a strangled moan. With each sound, his motion became more urgent until she was matching his loud moans. He rolled her onto her back, thrusting hard and desperate, forcing helpless cries from her. Their bellies slid together, slicked with sweat and heat. Her legs locked around his waist. "Marc," she yelled.

He pounded into her so hard the bed clanked against the wall. "Now, baby, scream."

Alex arched, the scream boiling up from her toes, unraveling her whole being as it went.

Marc shuddered and stopped, panting. "I knew you were a screamer."

Ugliness rolled through her like a dust storm. "Don't make fun."

"I'm not." He eased onto the bed beside her. "You always keep yourself from making any noise when we make love. You don't have to do that with me." He cupped her breast letting his thumb brush across her nipple. "I appreciate loud, so you can be who you are."

The ugliness vanished. He wasn't ridiculing her. He never had. "You can be yourself with me, too."

"I planned to. I'm not good at being anyone else."

"Like Jason."

He propped himself on his elbow. "What?"

"You said something about Jason writing a brilliant ballad. You've mentioned him before."

"I've had a long day, and I'm too tired for you to be smart right now." He stretched out beside her again and closed his eyes ending the discussion.

At least she wasn't the only screwed up person in this relationship.

Chapter 11

This bed had to go. Being this close to Alex was great, but every time he moved, he worried he was going to hurt her. He opened his eyes to watch her sleep. She hadn't brought up Jason again. After they napped, they'd made love again, and then she'd cooked some ramen because neither of them wanted to go down twenty flights of stairs or lose this private eyrie where she could scream.

He smiled. She was a screamer, and she had some wicked talent for sex. Last night when they made love at midnight, it was magic. Damn good thing she had that box of condoms.

She stretched and twisted toward him. "Good morning."

"Good morning."

"We have to go out today unless you want to eat ramen or Chef Boyardee for breakfast."

"Pack a bag, and we'll go to my hotel where the elevator works."

"I don't care as long as the bed works." She nuzzled her cheek against his chest.

"I can't have you dying of starvation now."

"I suppose not." Alex kicked her legs free of the sheet they were both entangled in and climbed off the bed. Standing in the middle of the room, she scrubbed her hands through her hair and then leered over her shoulder. "We could take a shower. There's no one here to walk in on us."

Marc stretched. "No, thanks. I'm still enjoying the smell of you on me. Maybe later."

She shrugged. "Your choice. I think we should go talk to Carla today. I'd like to get it over with. Plus, if we're at your hotel, Roger won't be able to hunt me down to pitch another hissy fit."

"Hissy fit?" Marc crossed the room so he could wrap his arms around her from behind. "You spent too much time with Ida this summer." Parts of his anatomy were waking up eager to continue last night's fun.

She reached up and behind to put her hand on the back of his head. "No, that I come by naturally. I did spend summers down there when I was little."

"You're still little." He nipped her shoulder.

The phone started to ring.

"Hold that thought." She slipped away.

"Just ignore it."

"Like you would." She picked up the handset of an ancient brown phone hanging on the wall. "Hello? Who? What? Yes, I hear them." She reached into a small metal chest of drawers and pulled out some underwear. Marc decided it would be wise to get dressed. "I'll be there as soon as I can."

"What's going on?"

"Screaming in the dean's office. Genesis said Dr. Meyer called Roger in to talk to him this morning first thing, and now Diana is there, too, and I could hear them yelling through the phone."

Marc dragged his shirt over his head. Yesterday's clothes, charming. Down twenty flights was easier than up and Alex went for the English building at a flat run.

"I didn't know what to do!" Genesis squealed as they came through the door. A boy, presumably Jeremy, stood to the right of the hall listening. "Dr. Meyer had me call Dr. Visian yesterday to come in for a meeting first thing, and then they started yelling, and Dr. Visian looks like he slept in his fruiting car. And then they had me call Dr. Gregor to come in immediately, and all three of them are screaming, and I heard your name so I looked your dorm phone number up in the department directory."

Genesis had followed Alex to the door of the dean's office, but stopped when Alex opened it. What to do? Stay out here with the kids or follow her in to where he didn't belong. Alex glanced back, catching his gaze, as she crossed the threshold and shook her head. Problem solved. Genesis retreated to reception and lingered on the left of the hall. Marc paced between the door and the couches below the window. Outside the sun shone and people carried on as if the world hadn't ground to a stop. From the dean's office, Marc could hear the occasional word or name. Impropriety and plagiarism were popular. So was Melanie Finch. He didn't hear Alex's voice at all.

They hadn't made any plans beyond breakfast yet. He'd thought he would find out what she wanted to do over eggs and bacon. Stay here and finish her degree or transfer to a school in L.A., or chuck it all and go to Italy. He'd been hoping for chuck it all so they could spend some time alone together before he had to subject her to the gang back home. They were going to be some fun now that he'd fallen in love at first sight, chased a woman across the country, and been documented all over Twitter searching for her. The band's forum was going to be a nightmare. Italy might be the only place to hide.

The screaming subsided. Marc leaned against the wall, toying words through his mind and tapping out a rhythm on his leg to pass the time. Genesis and Jeremy drifted away from their listening posts to get their work done, but they both kept looking back at the hall.

A blonde came out with Roger right on her heels, saying something about not telling anyone. He shot Marc a murderous look. Marc went to the mouth of the hall to wait for Alex. She had to come out. Where the hell was she?

The office door opened and Alex stepped out. She turned back, nodded, and came down the hall. Her face was pale. "Genesis, can you cancel all of the dean's appointments for the rest of the day. He's going to be leaving shortly. He's not feeling well."

"No fricking doubt."

"And he'd appreciate it if you didn't mention what happened here today. Either of you." She shot a look at Jeremy. "There's no need for anyone to know who was here, what was said, or what volume it was said at. If it goes around, the dean will have a fifty-fifty idea of who blabbed."

"We won't say a thing to a soul," Jeremy said.

Nice to know he could speak. Marc followed Alex out of the office and turned her toward the parking lot outside where his rental sat from yesterday with three tickets fluttering under the wiper blades. Alex pulled them out and ripped them in half.

"Don't I have to pay those?" Marc asked.

"What are they going to do, put a hold on your transcripts?" She climbed in the passenger side.

Marc slid into the driver's seat and plucked the torn tickets out of her hand. "Just the same. Are you going to tell me what happened?"

"This university is *Peyton Place*, and I don't care if I ever associate with these people again."

The words alone would have sounded so promising if it weren't for the dead tone of her voice. "So are we going to Italy?"

"I promised the dean I would finish my master's. He's going to be my advisor." She turned to him and her expression could have made Miss Mary Sunshine cry. "There is no way we can keep this under wraps. My master's defense is cancelled and then my advisor is changed to the dean of the school, and Melanie is still dead. It's all very fishy. This is all my fault."

"I thought you said Melanie jumped out her window during Christmas break."

"She did because Diana threatened to break up with her."

Marc started the car. "I think you need to start at the beginning."

"Diana was having an affair with Melanie, who was her assistant. Apparently, Melanie had written all or most of Diana's published papers for the past year and a half."

"That's criminal."

"I wrote several of Roger's."

Note to self: keep mouth shut with the judgmental announcements. That didn't constitute lying, did it?

"Anyway, Diana tried to break off the sex side of the relationship because she thought her husband was onto them."

"Her husband?" Damn it, what happened to keeping his mouth shut?

"I told you, *Peyton Place.* Diana told Melanie at the end of fall term that it was over between them and asked her to finish a paper over break."

Marc clenched his jaw. He pulled to a stop at a light.

"I know. That's fucked up, right?"

"The thought crossed my mind."

"Melanie didn't finish the paper and jumped out her window. Somehow Roger knew about this, and when I ended it with him, he went to Diana and told her she had to give him Melanie's thesis or he would tell the dean."

"About her and Melanie or about Melanie doing all her work?"

"One, the other, both. Wouldn't matter. Any of it could destroy her career."

"I thought you told the dean that you plagiarized the paper by accident."

"I did, but Roger assumed I had told Dr. Meyer the whole truth when I went to see him yesterday so he went in this morning guns blazing. He tried to throw it all on Diana, which was why she got called in. Now, all the dirty laundry is out. And it wouldn't be if I hadn't opened my big mouth."

Marc's stomach clenched. "How could you think any of this is your fault?"

"Because if I had just kept my mouth shut and gone through with the defense, I could have had my master's by"—she checked her watch—"about now, left for wherever with you, and everyone could have gone on with their lives."

"Their screwed up, highly dysfunctional lives. Honey, you have to listen to me on this. These kinds of things are never hidden forever." He put his hand on her thigh. "You've got teachers messing around with students, and students writing papers for teachers. Two people are cheating on their spouses, one opposite sex and one same sex just to make things equally unfair. Nobody was treading a gray area here. You didn't cause it, Alex. You got sucked into it, and you're a big damn hero for putting a stop to it."

"Where are we going?"

"My hotel."

"I need to talk to Carla."

Right now? "I figured you'd need a break between her and that scene in the office."

"No." Alex folded her hands in her lap. "I need to get this over with, and I want to tell her before Roger does."

"You think he will?"

"He's going to have to come up with some reason for this morning's summoning by the dean."

"How would she know about it?"

Alex rolled her eyes. "Genesis called Roger's house yesterday and left a message."

Hadn't she exacted a promise from Genesis and Jeremy to not say a word? How reliable was that going to be? "She didn't—"

"No, but she did say that Dr. Meyer wanted to see Roger first thing in the morning. Roger said that he and Carla got into a fight about it last night. That's how he ended up sleeping in his car."

Somewhere in the area a woman was coping with the fresh news that her husband had been cheating on her. Not good. "Tell me where to go."

Alex was stiff and quiet, only speaking to tell him where to turn. This was too much for her to cope with. The shit that fucker Roger put her through had been enough, but add this other bizarre wrinkle with the dead girl and the other cheating professor, and it was elevated beyond the average. Rock stars were supposed to be wild, and these people were putting Touchstone's party days to shame. When they were crazy, they'd had Sandy's very firm hand keeping them out of trouble, even if it meant threatening to quit managing the band, and they'd had each other to share the weight. He glanced at Alex, staring out the windshield and obviously not seeing the tree-lined street. Roger's wife deserved to know, but was it fair to make Alex do it face to face? She was young, and she made a mistake, but being the whistleblower had to be punishment enough.

Just because he wished somebody had told him about Dez didn't mean he had the right to force Alex into total disclosure. It was pretty brutal. Roger's wife was dealing with the truth, but his first priority had to be Alex. "Honey, you don't have to do this."

"Yes, I do."

He reached across the seat and tried to take her hand, but her fingers were so tightly laced together that he couldn't separate them, so he settled for resting his hand on her thigh. "There are other ways than telling her in person."

"But this is the right way. I was sleeping with her husband for three years. I need to apologize."

Three years? Three *years*? Marc swallowed his shock. The amount of time didn't matter as much as the fact that she'd ended it. Still, three years? "I understand the desire, but this is a much bigger can of worms than either of us anticipated."

"That's a cliché."

"What is?"

"Can of worms. Turn left at the next intersection."

"It's an appropriate cliché. If you really have to tell Carla, let it go a day."

"By then Roger will have sold her on whatever lie he's cooked up to cover this."

"Whether she believes you or not isn't the point. All you need to do is tell the truth, and you could do that in an e-mail."

"There's a VCS rental truck in Roger's driveway."

There was a truck with a familiar logo backed across the lawn to the porch of a brick house on the right. The front tires were sinking into a flowerbed of bright pink and white flowers along the driveway, but the rear tires were on the concrete walk so the truck wasn't stuck. He pulled into the driveway. Alex jumped out before he got the car in park.

"Carla?" She climbed the steps to the porch, but hesitated at the corner of the truck. "Carla?"

Marc bounded up the steps behind her. Who knew what this woman might do or be doing with a truck in the middle of her yard?

"Alex, is that you?" A petite reddish blonde came out of the kitchen, blowing her nose. "You heard?"

"Heard?"

"Roger was having an affair." Carla sobbed and wiped her W. C. Fields red nose again. "My family was right. They told me not to marry him. They told me if he'd cheat once, he'd cheat again, but Diana Gregor?

We had dinner with her and her husband. We all went to Disney World together last summer." Carla threw her hands up in the air. "I was probably babysitting her girls when she was screwing my husband. They were probably necking in the It's a Small World ride while we were in the boat in front with the kids."

"That's pretty unlikely," Marc muttered. Alex elbowed him.

"So you're leaving?" Alex asked.

Carla sunk down on a camel back sofa facing the fireplace, and Alex sat next to her. Marc leaned on the arm of a chair so he could dive in and pull the two women apart if he had to. Hell having no fury like a scorned woman and all. "We were out to dinner last night, and when we came home the sitter gave us a message from Dr. Meyer. He wanted Roger in his office first thing this morning on some allegations of plagiarism and impropriety. Plagiarism? Can you believe it? I asked Roger, and he had to confess." Carla wiped her nose again. "I just don't understand. I tried to be everything Vanessa wasn't."

"Vanessa?" Marc bit his tongue, but it was already out. Alex glared at him.

"Vanessa was his first wife," Carla said. "He was my freshman lit teacher, and he was so witty and charming. Vanessa was cruel, and she lied to him all the time. She promised him they would have kids as soon as she finished her doctorate, but then told him children would get in the way of her career. He so wanted a family." Carla's expression hardened. "Well, it's going to be a cold day in hell before he sees my children again." She got up and stormed into the kitchen. Alex stood to follow, but Marc stopped her.

"Wait, let me get this straight. Roger was married and cheated on his wife with Carla when she was in freshman English. Then he divorced wife one to marry Carla and started having an affair with you."

"Oh, what a tangled web we weave when we screw around with undergrads?" Alex shrugged and followed Carla into the kitchen.

"I'm keeping the dishes," Carla announced. "He can eat off paper plates for all I care. Can you help me wrap them? Or maybe I should smash the whole set in the driveway. What do you think?"

Marc positioned himself in the kitchen doorway, wondering where the knives were. Alex had been safer in the living room.

"I think…" Alex glanced at him. "I think I need to tell you something first."

Carla set down the plate in her hands. "Tell me it's not more bad news."

"Roger wasn't having an affair with Diana. He was having an affair with me."

Dear Lord, three women at the same time. If Roger wasn't such a creep, Marc thought he might admire the man. Why couldn't he have been juggling three careers at the same time? That would have been cool.

Carla blinked. "No, he was having an affair with Diana. He showed me the hotel receipts. That asshole had a credit card I didn't know about that he used for his illicit relationship."

"Where are your kids?" Marc asked. He should have thought of the kids before. They didn't need to hear this.

"Teri Lewiston has them while I pack." Carla waved toward the front of the house.

"Carla, I was having an affair with Roger," Alex repeated.

"It's very sweet of you to try to make me feel better, but it was Diana. I have proof. I printed out the history on that credit card. He's not getting a dime from me."

"A dime from you?" Marc asked.

"Daddy owns VCS."

"We used VCS on the first tour." Marc looked out the window. He remembered those huge rented semis packed with equipment on the road with them for thirteen months. That was why the logo was so familiar. "I didn't know they did little trucks, too."

"Trucks and drivers in all sizes."

"Carla," Alex said.

Marc grabbed her arm and yanked her out to the living room. "Let it go," he hissed.

"I have to tell her. It was me, not Diana."

"Apparently, it was both of you, and you did tell her. She just didn't believe you."

"She has to believe me."

"No, she doesn't. You told her. Your obligation is fulfilled. She can't handle the idea that her husband, who she got second hand from some other chick, was cheating on her with two other women."

"But he wasn't cheating with Diana, he was cheating with me."

"Did he take you to that hotel?"

"No, it was always in his office."

"Voila. He was cheating on his wife with you and cheating on you with this third—fourth woman. I'm starting to lose count."

Something shattered in the kitchen. Carla cursed and started to sob.

"But—"

"No, you need to trust me on this." Just like Carla didn't need the truth shoved down her throat, Alex didn't need to understand her beloved literature professor was nothing more than an alley cat looking to score with as many women as he could. It had been said, even if it didn't register. Like Helen had told him, there was no point in causing needless pain in the name of truth. "Let's just help her pack her shit and get out of here. Carla, should we just call some movers?" He went back into the kitchen.

Carla was taking dirty dishes out of the dishwasher and wrapping them in newspaper.

Marc lifted a marinara sauce covered plate out of her hands. "Let's run the washer before we pack these, hmm? We could call movers to load the van for you."

"Movers." Carla pressed the back of her wrist to her forehead. "Why didn't I think of that? I'll call the office. They'll send someone."

"And maybe another truck. It would be nice for Roger to come home to a house furnished with nothing but cobwebs." He started unwrapping the dirty dishes and loading the dishwasher.

* * * *

Alex walked into the hotel room and sat down on the foot of the bed. Seven hours spent helping Carla pack while a team of burly men and women loaded furniture and boxes into four trucks. Roger was left with a broken lawn chair and half a pair of chopsticks.

"Those guys were a trip." Marc closed the door. "It was like they took this personally. Her dad must be a great boss. I caught that guy Rosco upstairs unscrewing all the light bulbs, and Daisy with the Goth black hair wrapped up the soap from the bathrooms. Next time I have to move out on a woman, remind me to call them."

"Let's hope there isn't a next time." Alex should have had some kind of reaction to his comment, but she was too numb.

"Sorry, babe. That was a stupid thing to say." He sat down next to her and put his arm over her shoulders so she leaned her head on him.

Marc had taken the whole thing personally, too. It had been his suggestion to leave the broken lawn chair in the middle of the living room. Roger had not returned to the house before they left. Someone must have warned him to stay away.

"You okay?" Marc asked.

"No."

"How can I fix it?"

"You can't. I just don't know what to think, and all the decisions have been taken out of my hands." She blinked and her eyes burned, either from anguish or dust. It didn't matter. Both options would produce tears, and she still wouldn't have any control.

"Did you eat any of the pizza I ordered around lunchtime? It's going on dinner now, anyway. I'll order room service." He stood up.

"I'm not hungry."

"You should eat."

"I don't want anything."

He knelt on the floor in front of her. "Alex, honey, I've been where you are. I've listened to my own footsteps because there weren't any footsteps with mine. I've said I can't do this anymore, but stayed because I didn't have anywhere to go. You aren't trapped. You have options."

"I'm not upset about losing Roger."

"That's good to hear."

Smartass. "But I have to work alongside him for the next year, at least while I finish my master's."

"I thought he wasn't your advisor anymore."

"He's not, but he's going to be there. He's tenured."

"So transfer to another school. You have to be able to finish this thing somewhere else."

"I have to stay here."

"Why?"

"I promised the dean."

"I think he'd understand. What do you want to do?"

"I can't do what I want to do."

"Hey, you're riding with me now, and I'm a goddamn skylight." He grinned.

Laughter bubbled through her chest, almost painful. Every muscle in her body ached.

Marc picked her up and carried her to the head of the bed where he cuddled around her. "In a perfect world, what would you want?"

"For dinner?"

"For the rest of your life."

Alex bit her lip. She'd spent so long jumping from one terrible choice to another like they were rocks across a river that to have anything possible made her a little queasy. "I'm so close. I'd like to finish my master's, and I'm committed to another year in the dorm."

"Is that what you want or what you feel like you have to do?"

Alex closed her eyes. How the hell was she supposed to know? She thought that's what she wanted. That was going to have to be good enough for now. "It's what I want."

"Okay, for the next year, you will live in your dorm and I'll get a place in town."

"You don't have to go to work or anything?"

"My buddy's wife is having a baby so he won't be going anywhere until a couple of months after the kid is born. We might be recording in West Virginia next summer, but not before, and I could drive between here and there. Shep and I should be able to do most of his solo album through e-mail. If not, it might be a couple of days here and there, but I want to spend as much time as possible with you. So you'll get your degree, and we'll go to Italy next summer."

"It never occurs to you that I might not want you here."

"No. Don't you?"

"I do, but I've never met anyone quiet so confident before."

"Welcome to a brave new world, sugar." He nuzzled her neck. "What about marriage? Is that something you want?" His arms tightened around her.

She had never planned and replanned her wedding, but Marc she could trust to be there forevermore. "It is, but when are we going to fit it in?"

"After the school year ends and before Italy."

How could he sound so nonchalant about it? "I can't plan a wedding while writing and preparing to defend my thesis. I don't even know what I want."

"Candy will do the planning, just talk to her about what you want. She's done several already."

All these people she was going to have to get to know. They might not like her. Marc could lose interest in three months. Then all of this would have been for naught. She snuggled into him with a comfortable sigh. No, he wouldn't lose interest. "I want kids. But not too soon."

"A year here, Italy, recording, and a tour. Is two or three years from now good enough?"

"I was thinking I'd wait until I was thirty."

"I'm not excited about being in my fifties with babies. We'll discuss it after we get through this year."

She twisted to look at his face. "Isn't it a little creepy to plan like this?"

"What's creepy is planning and not being willing to adjust for circumstances. We might not get to Italy next year. Recording and touring might come up sooner than I expect. Are you going to kill me if that happens?"

"No, but I'll pout and demand that you buy me ice cream." She turned to press her back against his chest. There were index cards taped to the wall beside the bed with lengths of yarn connecting them. "What the hell is that? Were you conducting a manhunt?"

"Sort of. You left me, and then you dumped me. I needed to know why."

Some of the players were there, including a few from West Virginia. A couple of direct quotes missing their proper punctuation. "You're missing a few people."

"I didn't have a complete playbook, but I still figured it out. I got to Roger."

Alex studied the mind map on the wall. Somehow, it was comforting to see that he'd invested all that time and effort into figuring her out after she'd told him to go. It shouldn't have. Roger hadn't been able to let go, but he'd hunted her down and manipulated her into staying with him. Marc just needed to know and wanted the best for her. She tugged his arms tighter around her. He put her interest ahead of his own.

"Is there any way we can keep that?"

"Why?"

She smiled. Why? That obsessive crazed thing on the wall was better proof of love than anything she'd ever seen. It wasn't big bands and grand passion, but Marc hadn't been willing to let anyone put her in a corner.

Epilogue

"Ah, *scusi*?" The man in front of her fumbled with a map. A woman Alex presumed to be his wife stood a couple of feet behind him frowning and staring down the Grand Canal. "This— this *vaporatto* go, go—via—um—Rialto Bridge?"

"I speak English," Alex said.

"Thank God." The man melted a little. His wife also sighed. "I can't make heads or tails of this map. Can you tell me how to get to the Rialto Bridge from here?"

Alex glanced over her shoulder at Marc. No wonder tourists thought she was a local with Marc glued to his phone all the time. "You need the *vaporatto* on the other side of the canal."

"How do we get there?"

Alex pointed. "Footbridge."

"Can you answer me another question?"

Marc slid his phone back in his pocket and draped his arm over Alex's shoulders. The man frowned at Marc. It was the now familiar don't-I-know-you expression.

"My girlfriend and I were wondering what all the padlocks are about."

"The Love Locks on the bridges? You put a padlock on a bridge and throw away the key. It means you and your lover will never split up."

Marc kissed her temple. They had discussed getting a Love Lock, but hadn't done it yet.

"Aren't you Marc Wells?" the girlfriend asked.

"I am."

"Can I have your autograph?" She snatched the map out of the man's hand and started riffling through her purse.

"Hey!" the man said. "We need that."

"We'll get another one."

Alex held out a pen. She'd learned after the first month to have a couple on her every time she went out with Marc. People at school had eventually gotten over Marc Wells sightings, but everywhere else he was stopped and people didn't usually have a pen they could find right away. She should start carrying around a notebook, too. Marc released Alex and autographed their map across a restaurant ad.

"Can I take a selfie with you, too?" The girlfriend was bouncing on her toes. The man looked like he wanted to throw Marc in the canal.

Marc obliged for the selfie, smiling stiffly. "You guys have a good trip." He guided Alex in the opposite direction of the footbridge.

"Where are you taking me?"

"Away from the fan. Look, the boat is coming. We can ride out to the gardens." He turned her in to the shelter at the *vaporatto* stop and wrapped his arms around her waist. "So what do you think? Will they make it?"

"Are you kidding? Did you see the looks that guy was giving you? If he doesn't learn to control his jealousy, and she doesn't learn to stop slobbering all over the nearest rock star, they don't have much of a future."

Marc nodded. "I concur."

"So what's up with Suzi?"

"She's in Potterville with Brian."

Alex smirked. Didn't take a genius to see that one coming. "Really now?"

"Yeah, there's a picture of them near Ida's. I wonder what she's doing there."

"You're kidding, right?"

"No."

The boat docked and Alex and Marc joined the line to climb on. "Brian has a huge crush on Suzi, and Suzi has a thing for Brian."

"He does not. He's just been worried about her like all of us have been. I was with him in Japan when she broke up with Logan."

"You are such a man sometimes."

"Good thing for you." He pulled her against him.

"What do you want to do after this?"

"After the garden or after Venice?"

So many options. Alex rubbed her cheek against his sweater. "How long do you plan to stay in Italy?"

"As long as you like, Mrs. Wells." He kissed her nose and then turned to watch the city slide past the windows.

Last year, while he waited for her to finish her masters, he and Glen had recorded an album in Chicago and then traveled back and forth to

Potterville to record with his own band. Marc felt bad about leaving her alone so much that he was perfectly happy to go wherever she wanted now that both records were finished. "We could take a train to Rome."

"I'll tell the concierge to set it up when we get back to the hotel."

The boat bumped into a dock, but it wasn't the right one yet so Alex indulged in watching tourists scramble off, and then onto, the *vaporatto*. The longer they stayed in Italy, the longer she could put off getting too involved with all of Marc's friends in California. A lot of people were surprised she didn't know most of them by reputation. Moving to Los Angeles might require as much preparation as her thesis defense and wedding combined.

"Suzi doesn't have a thing for Brian. They're just good friends. Brian's her biggest fan," Marc said.

"You are welcome to believe that, but it isn't true."

"Present your evidence."

"She calls him several times a week to have long conversations."

"She calls me several times a week." The boat unmoored and set off across open water toward the garden.

"But she doesn't talk about talking to you. When I hear from her it's 'How's the thesis coming? Send me anything you want me to proof. I was talking to Brian, and on and on.'"

"So she does talk about me."

Alex snapped her fingers in front of his eyes. "Hey, Mr. Center of the World, back on topic."

"But she does talk about me."

"To me, but it makes sense that she would talk to me about you. It doesn't make sense that she would talk to me about Brian. Candy says she talks to her about Brian, too."

"You and Candy got very chummy."

"She was planning my wedding. We had to talk." Plus Candy was nice and it would be good to know somebody when she landed in California permanently. The wedding reception had been a blur of names and faces that she half knew and hoped she wouldn't be quizzed on.

"What are you going to do now that you're finished with your degree?" Marc asked. "I'm going to be on tour in a few months and we're usually on the road six weeks, then home for two over the course of about eight months."

The boat bumped against the garden dock giving her a minute to collect herself. Another good reason to stay in Italy as long as she could.

Going home meant dealing with having nothing to do for the first time in her life.

They walked in silence to the public park. The wide gravel paths and trees didn't fit with her image of Venice, and that's why she liked it here so much. These quiet surprises.

"Maureen and Cassie join us on tour sometimes. Cassie won't be this time, not with the baby, but if you wanted, you could. Then you and Maureen could go site seeing while we're working. Maureen also volunteers in the school. Candy and Tessa have a gym they go to. Not that you need a gym."

"I'm not going to run away with my personal trainer."

"I didn't say that."

Alex smirked at him. "You didn't have to." She laced her fingers through his. They had passed through the meandering park area to the long path that lead back to town. After the narrow alleys and crowded streets of Venice, this felt very exposed. "I don't know what I'm going to do. I had planned to get my masters and apply to a doctorate program, but I'm not sure that's what I ever really wanted to do. The doctorate was just so I could work with Roger. Did I tell you Roger is teaching remedial English at a community college in Birmingham, Alabama?"

"Several times."

The path ended on a street that was two lanes wide. Two little Oriental girls rode past on bikes chattering in Italian.

"Gelato?" Marc asked.

"Sure." Alex waited on the street as Marc went for the gelato. Since she was a kid, she'd been busy. School and clubs, then school and work, any time gaps filled with reading, mostly of the dry academic type as she tried to get ahead or impress someone. She hadn't read for fun in years, and the only movies she'd watched had been with Marc. All that time she'd spent making fun of Finn and his parade of police dramas? She hadn't seen any of them.

"Here you go. Strawberry. Your favorite." Marc handed her a cone.

"I have not seen a single episode of *Castle*."

"Okay, and what is this stemming from?" Marc licked his cone. His gelato looked too dark to be hazelnut.

"You asked me what I wanted to do now, and I realized I've missed a lot of television and movies and books because I've been studying."

"You read Suzi's books."

"Only because you had them on your e-reader on the flight over here."

"So you're going to become a consumer of popular culture full time?"

"For a while. You got a problem with that?"

He draped his arm over her shoulders. "As a producer of popular culture, I have no problem with that at all."

Meet the Author

Born in Northeast Ohio, I have lived on four different continents (including both sides of Asia) and traveled extensively. I have an extremely elaborate fantasy life and have forgotten that my bands don't really exist to the extent that I have shooped for their albums on iTunes. I have met sheikhs, magnates, high ranking politicians and the guy who did the original production paintings for Raiders Of the Lost Ark, but I'm pretty sure the only celebrity who would make me completely tongue tied would be Randolph Mantooth of Emergency!

Join my mailing list http://eepurl.com/4VZuD

Visit Christa at http://www.kensingtonbooks.com/author.aspx/29516

Turn the page for a special excerpt of Christa Maurice's

Satellite of Love

They love each other. Will the rest of the world let them?

Reluctantly on her way to a blind date, Maureen detours to her mechanic thanks to squeaky. He's not there, but his intriguing brother is. Maureen can't believe how instantly and powerfully she's attracted to this grease monkey. But since Michael is only town for a week, she doesn't want to waste an instant.

Michael is no grease monkey. He's Bear D'Amato, rock n' roll drummer. He's leaving in a week to get ready for a world tour with his band, Touchstone. When he first meets Maureen, he just wants to have some fun. But when relationship deepens, he realizes he wants more than just a couple of dates. He wants a lifetime.

On sale now!

http://www.kensingtonbooks.com/book.aspx/31377

Chapter 1

Maureen dropped her head to the steering wheel in front of Tony's Garage. She was not going to make that blind date, and depending on the repair bill, might be happy about that. One of these days she had to tell her friend Linda no when she came up with another man. So far they had all been wasted evenings.

She really needed to try to meet some decent men on her own. So far the strategy of school all day and sitting home all night planning for school the next day wasn't working so great for the social calendar.

At least the screaming brakes gave her a good excuse to cancel. The sign said closed, but when she pushed the door, it opened. The bay to the right was empty, but further back, in the bays behind the building, she could hear clanking and a radio playing. Tony must be working late.

"Hello?" Maureen peered through the short hallway from the obsessively clean waiting area to the back repair bays. The far door stood nearly closed so she could only see a sliver of the room. A tire, a black fender with a piece of masking tape on it, a work light, a black hood propped open. "Tony? Are you back there? It's Maureen Donnelly."

Feet shuffled and the radio's volume lowered. What if it wasn't Tony? Maybe one of his assistants had stayed late. Rusty or...the high school kid...Eric, that was his name. Did Tony trust his high school work-study assistant enough to leave him alone in the garage after hours? "I'm having some trouble with my brakes. They're making a lot of noise. You probably heard them when I pulled in."

What if it wasn't either one of them? What if it was some total stranger? What if it was somebody dangerous? She fumbled in her purse for her cell phone then stopped.

What was she going to do? Call 911 so they could listen to her screams for help without being able to do anything because they didn't know where she was? Tomorrow's headline could read: *Second Grade*

Teacher Slain In Garage, Too Stupid To Know Responders Couldn't Track Her Cellphone Signal. She should have gotten one of those apps that broadcast her every move. Then she could have just posted to Facebook. *Being murdered. Call Police. Tony's Garage.*

The door to the back bays opened and a bulky silhouette that didn't really fit Tony, Rusty, or Eric filled it.

She took a step back toward the outside door. "Hi, sorry I bothered you. I can come back in the morning." *Teacher's Body Found Rolled In Rug Behind Convenience Store, Cell Phone Still In Her Hand.*

"It's okay." The man walked through the dark hall and into the waiting area. His broad, friendly face seemed familiar. He wore his long brown hair in a ponytail and had a smudge of grease on his cheek. "I heard you pull in. You want me to take a look?"

"No." She bumped into the door. "I mean, you don't have to. I'll just leave it for Tony in the morning." The mechanic didn't look at all threatening, but adrenalin interfered with rational thought. *Memorial Service For Murdered Teacher Tuesday, Local Garages Offering Free Brake Checks. Says Tony D'Amato, owner of the garage where her car was found Friday, "If she'd just gotten that squeaking noise checked when she first heard it, all of this could have been avoided."*

"They sounded pretty bad. You might have worn down to the rotors. Let me take a look." He crossed the room.

Honestly, he looked about as threatening as the Easter Bunny. If the Easter Bunny had amazing shoulders. "It's okay." Before she announced that someone was picking her up, she stopped herself. The neighborhood wasn't the greatest and calling for a ride meant standing around in it, increasing her chances for ending up in that rug. Better the devil she had just met than the one who might be lurking in the dark. "Who are you?"

He had been reaching out, hopefully to grab the door because his hands were filthy, but pulled back when she asked. "I'm— I'm Michael, Tony's brother."

"Michael. No wonder you look familiar. Sorry. I wasn't sure." Too much caffeine and too many murder mysteries. She needed to lay off both for a while.

"That's okay." Michael pursed his lips. Nice lips they were too. Full, red, very kissable for the Easter-Bunny-slash-killer. "You want me to take a look at those brakes now?"

"Sure. Thanks. I know it's after hours, but they started to sound really bad." She held out her keys. "I guess you'll need to put it up on the lift or something."

Michael nodded, ripped some paper off the roll inside the door to protect the interior of her precious ten-year-old clunker and crossed the lot to her car. She wouldn't mind having that body in her driver's seat. The way he filled out his coverall was a sight. Broad shoulders, narrow waist, nice tight butt. Very nice.

She turned away from the window before he caught her staring. Good thing she wasn't going on that date in this frame of mind. From murdered and rolled in a rug to sweaty sex on the hood of a car in ten seconds flat, and all she'd needed was his name.

Oh. Date.

Her phone was still in her hand so she located the latest bachelor on her list of calls as she walked through the hallway to watch Michael pull her car in. Tony didn't like customers in the bay. He claimed it was dangerous. The only danger she could imagine was brain damage from the stench of oil, gasoline and exhaust. Brain damage be damned, she wasn't going to pass on the chance to ogle.

"Hello?"

"Hi—" Crud, what was this bachelor's name? "It's Maureen. I wanted to let you know I can't make it tonight."

"Sorry to hear that." He didn't sound sorry. Maybe Linda's sales pitch hadn't been that good.

"My brakes are making a horrible noise. I'm sure you can hear it." Michael had just pulled through the door and the squeals echoed beautifully on the cinderblock walls.

"That sounds pretty bad. Um... I guess you'll need a ride."

"No." That was it. No more of Linda's blind dates. "I'll be fine."

"Okay. I guess I'll talk to you."

Not if I recognize your number before I answer the phone. "Yeah. Okay. 'Bye." She closed her phone. At this very moment she could be at home watching TV in sweats, grading math tests and deciding to bring the car to Tony tomorrow. She'd washed her hair, shaved her legs, put on makeup and dressed up for whatshisname. The sexy dark blue jersey dress she'd selected needed somebody who'd appreciate her effort. Hands on hips to hold her coat open, she sauntered behind the car. Michael was operating the lift, but he gave her a once over when she passed.

"Well?" she asked.

"They aren't supposed to sound like that. I'll have to pull the tire off to see how bad it is, but it's not going to be good. Does Tony do all the maintenance on your car?"

"Most of it. He told me to go to the quick lube places for my oil changes." Lube, hehe. She really needed to mix with adults more often.

"Has your transmission fluid been clear?" Michael walked to the front driver's side tire, so she followed him.

"I guess so. The guy at the lube place said I needed to have it flushed next time I go in. Why?"

"Felt to me like your transmission was slipping." He popped the hubcap off and used a loud tool to loosen the lug nuts.

When she flinched away from the noise, she bumped into the car he'd been working on. It was black except for the trunk, which was orange. Just sitting there, hood up and orange trunk lid, it seemed to say, "Hey, baby, wanna ride?" She sidled toward the front. On the fender a strip of masking tape said *Satellite of Love*. "Is this your car?"

Michael looked over his shoulder, yanking the tire off as if it weighed less than a duvet. "Yeah. That's my baby."

"Satellite of Love?"

"My sister-in-law's idea of a joke. It's a '72 Plymouth Satellite."

As if that meant something to her. As far as she could tell, it was a car that might or might not run. She leaned on the Satellite's fender. Her car always looked so helpless up on the lift. More so now that it was missing a tire.

"You headed someplace tonight?" Michael asked.

"A date."

"Sorry."

"Naw, if I'd really wanted to be there I could have continued to ignore that squealing." She grinned, but he didn't turn around to see it. Another wasted effort. "So what are you doing here?"

"I'm visiting my brother and his family." Michael glanced over his shoulder frowning, clearly absorbed with the car thing in his hand. Men and their obsession with inanimate objects. "This is bad."

"What's bad?" She stepped forward.

"This piece?" He held up a dirty, holey piece of who knew what in his large, strong-looking hand. "This is the shoe. This is what stops your car and it works best when it isn't full of holes."

Her grimace, such an attractive expression, he did see. Of course. "Is it expensive?"

"Expensive?"

Why did he sound like money was no object to him? "Yes, is it going to cost a lot to fix?"

"It's not cheap, but it's a lot less expensive than plowing into a wall or another car." He shrugged. "Tony's pretty busy tomorrow, but if he can't get to it, I'm sure we can do it Sunday so you can have it back for Monday."

She clenched her fists behind her back. As if that would keep the money from flying out of her wallet. "Will somebody call me and tell me when to bring it in?"

"Oh no." Michael dropped the worn brake shoe on the floor. "You can't drive out of here like this."

"If you put the tire back on, I can."

"No, you can't." Michael folded his arms, which accented those fantastic shoulders and did incredible things to the muscles in his upper arms. "I can't let you drive this car in good conscience. You'd be a danger to yourself and anyone else on the road."

"Great." Maureen stared out the bay door into the waning light, thoughts of fantastic shoulders ebbing. She'd have been better off going on the stupid date. A whole weekend without a car? The price was too high. "How am I supposed to get home?"

"I can give you a ride or you can call a cab."

Her stomach growled. On the top of her To Do list for tomorrow was buying groceries. Until she could get out to the store, she was eating oatmeal and crackers with jelly. "Great."

"You know, if you're hungry we could stop for pizza on the way." Michael smiled. He had a warm, playful smile that gave her a glimpse of the little boy in this big hunk of man. "My treat since I know Tony is going to gouge you on the repair. I'll even kick in a ride in the Satellite of Love."

Well, that did make the bill a little more manageable. "You had me at pizza."

He nodded. "I'm known for overplaying my hand. Let me clean up and we'll get out of here." Switching off the work light hooked to the Satellite, he set it aside and closed the hood. Then he headed toward the little hallway. "It'll only take me a minute."

This had to be one of her more irrational moments. Fifteen minutes ago she'd been convinced he was going to murder her and dump her body in an alley and now they were headed out to grab a pizza? In his car yet. Insane much? "Hey, you aren't going to turn out to be a serial killer, are you?" she called after him.

He turned at the mouth of the hallway. "A what?"

"Never mind."

He chuckled, a deep rich sound. "Don't worry. I'm not a serial killer." Then he ducked through a door in the hall that was always closed.

She should probably be concerned about the way he emphasized the word *not*, but somehow couldn't summon the desire.

No, she was busy desiring something else.

* * * *

Bear stripped off his coveralls and hung them on the door of the extra locker. He'd been hoping to get a little more work done on the Satellite, but this was a lot more interesting. Pulling on the Tesla t-shirt he'd worn in this morning, he wished he'd dressed a little better. Of course, Maureen Donnelly thought he was an auto mechanic, so the old concert t-shirt and jeans might be a better way to sell the illusion.

His phone had five messages. One from Sandy, one from Candy, one from Jason and two from Marc. Sandy was probably mad he hadn't called in since last week. Going off the radar like he had, especially with a tour looming, must be driving Sandy nuts. Candy wanted him to do some publicity thing. Her job was getting them publicity, but she never had understood the word *vacation*. Jason, if Jason was still acting the way he had been for the past couple of weeks since he'd gotten dumped in *People*, was just calling to bitch. He called Marc and pinned the phone between his shoulder and ear while he scrubbed grease off his fingers.

"Yo."

"What?"

"Nothin'. When are you coming back?"

"Ten days." He checked his watch as if it measured days. Ten short days, until he was stuck in a room, and then a series of rooms, with the rest of the band and their melodrama.

"Good. Jason is selling the New York apartment."

"Beautiful, so he's going to be in Malibu all the time now?"

"I guess. Ty has taken up grass boarding."

"What the fuck is that?"

"Just like snowboarding, but on grass."

"He can still sing when he falls and fucks up his wrists. Did you call for a reason or just to give me a newsy update?"

"Why? You got a hot date or something?"

Bear didn't answer. He'd hoped to already be tooling down the road with Maureen Donnelly headed for a simple pizza between two people who'd just met. Two totally normal people.

"The suits just want to make sure everything is on track," Marc said. "The album is still moving up the charts but the single is slipping. The next single is coming out Tuesday and it would really help if you would pick up a little promo."

"I'm. On. Vacation."

"I know, but we owe the company a fortune and if this record tanks, we are never going to record another one. The label will drop us and we'll all end up managing a fast food joint."

"Yeah, I know. I took Rock Star 101 with you." His head started to throb. "We did all that promo when the album came out. The thing for MTV and that Canadian show. And we're doing that casino to kick off the tour. All I asked for was two fucking weeks."

"And all I'm asking you to do is take two hours out of your vacation and hit a radio station."

"Marc, they're getting the next ten months of my life."

"It's the job, man, and it's the best fucking job in the world." Marc's tone remained pleasant and even.

"I know. Is that what Sandy wanted?"

"No, Sandy wants to know where you are and that you're healthy."

"Tell him I'm right where I was the last time he talked to me and in about the same shape."

"Great. Jason has been busting his ass on promo."

The last thing he wanted to hear about was what a superhero Jason was. Not with a sweet thing like Maureen Donnelly waiting. "I gotta go."

"Oh, that's right. The hot date. See ya in ten days."

Bear snapped his phone closed as he pulled on his leather jacket. He should have skipped this whole music thing and gone into business with his brother.

Then both of them could be trying to scratch a living out of this little three bay garage.

He snatched the keys off the locker shelf and hurried out to see if Maureen Donnelly had hung around while he was getting scolded.

She stood in the filthy repair bay behind her car, holding her purse with both hands. Cocking her head, she gave him a little smile.

For about ten seconds, he couldn't take his eyes off her. The minimal makeup she wore accented the simple prettiness of her features instead of them being obliterated under raccoon eyeliner and some wild shade of lipstick. Her brunette hair was cut in a bob and pulled back off her face. He hadn't seen what with yet, but he bet it was a bow or some kind of flower. The dark blue dress crisscrossed over her perfect, unenhanced bust, creating some really intriguing cleavage.

Really intriguing. He couldn't see her legs around the bumper of the car, or her shoes. He wanted to check out her shoes and, more importantly, the legs that led into them. As he recalled, the hem fell right to her knees.

"Sorry I took so long." He tore his gaze away from where he could have seen her legs if he had x-ray vision, and met hers. She didn't seem to be on to him. "I had to make a call."

"No problem." She shook her head and her cute little bob bounced around her shoulders.

"I'll lock up and we can go." He ducked into the waiting room to lock the door and turn off the lights. The sooner he got out of here, the sooner he was going to get a look at her legs. "Which pizza place do you like better? Napoli or Mama Lena's? I like Napoli's."

"So do I, but I don't like to eat there." She sounded sorry as she followed him to the car door.

He glanced over his shoulder. Her pretty, small mouth was drawn into a frown. "Why?"

"They're always screaming at each other, did you notice? The food is wonderful, but the brothers who own the place are always arguing or yelling at the kids waiting tables." She shivered. "It just makes me uncomfortable."

"Tony always gets carry out. I guess there's a reason." He opened the passenger door of the Satellite. "Mama Lena's it is."

She sat down on the seat sideways and twisted forward like a lady. His mom used to get into cars that way when she wore a dress and he'd never seen any other woman do it. Swallowing at the unfamiliar rush of mixed heat and uncertainty, he opened the bay door so he could back out. This woman was not a score-seeking groupie. Maureen Donnelly qualified as a nice girl.

And he was already lying to her.

Not lying really, but not filling her in on a few details. Like he wasn't an auto mechanic and in a couple of weeks, he'd be off on the one ring circus currently known as the Bayonet Ball Tour. Like the next time she saw him after this, he'd probably be on MTV. If she even watched that. She struck him as a History Channel type.

Did it really matter? He was taking her out for a pizza, not marrying her. For one night, he could just be Michael, the guy who was buying her a pizza, taking her home and maybe getting a kiss on the doorstep instead of Bear D'Amato, drummer for Touchstone.

He backed the car out and closed the garage door. "So what is it you do?"

"I'm a teacher. I teach second grade at Wilson."

"Really?" Teacher. Little kid teacher yet. That fit. "You like it?"

"Yeah, it's great, but I'm looking forward to summer vacation."

"Oh?"

"February is kinda long and Spring Break is late this year so we've had this really long stretch with no days off. It gets a little tiring, for the teachers and the kids."

"I always thought the teachers were annoyed when we had days off." He glanced at her. She had half turned toward him with her purse in her lap, as if she were interested in the conversation, not as if she were amortizing him.

"Nope. We're all shooing the kids out the door and making plans for our days off."

"And what do you like to do on your days off?" What did regular people do on their days off? Most of his time was spent in the studio, on tour or in between and in between was only a couple of days here and there. Not that it was bad, he did have the greatest job in the world, but it was a twenty-four seven gig. Even last year's sabbatical had been spent analyzing what had gone wrong with the previous album so they could avoid it this time.

"The usual stuff. I read, watch TV, garden a little."

"Go out on blind dates."

She groaned. "Yeah. I should have given that up for Lent. My friend Linda means well, but she's not very good at it. I think next time I'm going to be washing my hair or something pressing like that."

"So it is an excuse."

"Like you've ever gotten it."

"Once or twice." A long time ago. Now all he had to do was pick a girl from the line up, which was frustrating in its own way.

Her laugh was light and musical. "So what do you do, other than fix cars?"

Damn. How to answer this question without flat out lying? "I travel and play music." That sounded good. Like they were two separate things.

"Travel. I've always wanted to travel, but never had the money. Where have you been?"

"All over." He clenched the steering wheel. He'd never seen much of the places he'd been. Travel, perform, sleep, repeat.

"That sounds wonderful."

Not the word he'd use. "So you have a garden?"

"Yeah. I bought a house last year so I spent last summer gardening. I'm really looking forward to my tulips and daffodils coming up this spring."

He pulled into the parking lot of Mama Lena's. The place was jammed. Great, now he had to use his fame to pull a few strings for a table, blowing his cover, or stand around like a jerk waiting for one. "Here we are."

"Wow, they're busy tonight." She checked her watch. "Let's hope the theater at the mall has a showing time soon so we don't have to wait long. I don't know about you, but I'm starved."

Oh yeah, she would *expect* to wait for a table. She wouldn't be disappointed when he couldn't magically make one open up for her. Man, he was so out of practice for this regular dating thing.

She climbed out without waiting for him to open her door and strode toward the restaurant, giving him the chance to fall back and check out the rear view, what he could see of it above and below her black raincoat. Her calves were slender and well shaped, practically insuring fantastic legs. The three-inch heels she wore put a beautiful glide in her stride. Her hair clip wasn't a bow or flowers. It was a gold Mickey Mouse. Mickey freakin' Mouse. This woman was so real, she was surreal.

He pulled open the door. Nobody lingered in the tiny waiting area and a blonde in a white t-shirt and black pants with a little red waitress's apron wrapped around her waist bounded over before the door even fell shut.

"Hi, Miss Donnelly, you need a table? Benny's clearing one now." The waitress's gaze shifted over Maureen's shoulder and her eyes went wide. He had about ten seconds before his cover went up in hysteria.

"Thanks, Tara. How's your sister doing?" Maureen scanned the restaurant. When she returned to the waitress, the girl's gaze pinged back to her, still wide eyed.

"My sister? Um, Ellie's fine. Um... I'll, um...check on Benny." The waitress spun around and all but sprinted for the back of the restaurant. Probably headed for the kitchen where she would tell the entire staff he was here.

"Tara's little sister was in my class two years ago." Maureen turned and frowned. "You have grease on your face."

"I do?" Bear watched over her shoulder for the kitchen staff to come boiling through the swinging doors to check out the visiting celebrity.

"Yeah. Do you want a Kleenex?" She dug in her purse.

"No, I'll just go wash it off in the bathroom." He lunged past her in the direction the waitress had gone, crossed the dining room without touching the floor and burst into the kitchen.

The entire staff huddled around Tara. They turned as a unit to stare at him. All of them in Touchstone's target audience range.

"I told you!" Tara shrieked.

"Hush," an older man hissed. The only one not in the crowd. "The customers will hear you."

"Listen, I just want to have a nice quiet dinner." Bear held up his hands. "I'll sign all the autographs you want in here, but out there I'd really appreciate it if you treated me like anybody else."

"But you're not anybody else," a girl with black hair and black rimmed glasses whimpered. "You're Bear D'Amato from Touchstone."

"You know Brian Ellis," another girl said.

"And Jason Callisto."

That broke their spell and they rushed him, order tablets out for autographs, babbling about how much they liked the album and the single and were they going to be doing a show anyplace close? He started signing. "I'm going to be in town for a few more days and I really want to keep it quiet. I just want to have dinner like anybody else. If everyone could just keep this between us until I leave, maybe I can talk the band into swinging by here while we're on tour. But seriously, if there's a breath of a rumor that I'm here, I can't promise anything."

The whole group gasped, exchanging conspiratorial glances. Hopefully, it would be as easy to arrange as it had been to promise. Sandy was going to murder him.

Tara stood in front of him with bright eyes. "Are you dating Miss Donnelly?"

"I'm having dinner with Miss Donnelly." Eventually. If he ever managed to get back to her. He'd been gone a really long time and still had grease on his face.

"I bet she doesn't even know who you are." Tara clutched her autograph to her chest. "She's so tragically unhip. I'll go seat her."

"Not a word," he cautioned as she scooted through the door. Now he was lying. Flat out, no doubt, lying.

But if he told her, she'd either run screaming or latch on tighter for all the wrong reasons. He just wanted one night. Not even the whole night. For the next three hours, he wanted to be nobody special.